Christmas at S Cottage

CW00417902

Karlie Parker

DEDICATION

For Poppy, Max, Casey, Darcy and Ross. Oh, and Gareth, who hates
dedications unless they mean something. Thank you!

CONTENTS

ACKNOWLEDGMENTS

Thanks to all of my family, Casey, Darcy, Ross, Poppy, Max and Les.
A big thanks to Gareth Davies, who kindly edited this. His insight and ideas
made the book you are reading!

Thanks to my yogi friends, and my sister friends, Kate, Sinem, and Ozzie, and
my actual sister, Lisa. And my many lovely brothers and Mum xx

At the other end of the phone, my best friend Mairi squealed with appalled delight.

"You did not!"

"Oh, I did," I said, heaving the box of my desk items up onto my hip and breathing in the fresh air outside the office building. I looked up towards the imposing offices of JD Banff and Partners, my employers. Make that *former* employers.

"Unintentionally of course."

Mairi sucked in a deep breath and then sighed it out as a laugh.

"Isla! This is too much! They are funny emails but I thought they were for my eyes only. I'm still laughing at what you said about Phil in that last one."

She was right of course. They were meant to be silly observations, not for anyone to see.

This morning, after I'd been sent on not one but *two* coffee runs for my manager, I'd accidentally CC'd my letter of resignation to the whole office.

"Emergency trip?" Mairi said when she eventually stopped laughing.

The emergency trip was a pact we'd created when we were young. If the other needed anything, all we had to say was those two little words and the other vowed to be there as quickly as they could and give their undivided attention for as long as possible. The last time we'd used it was when I'd popped into Marks and Spencer to try on some Spanx in my lunch hour and, having got them on, spent forty minutes trying to get them off again. By the time Mairi arrived, I'd managed to fight my way free and met her red-faced outside. I bought the offending article, of course, but later stuffed it into a drawer at the back of my closet and never looked at it again.

Did this need an emergency trip?

As a marketing manager, I'd had hopes of this job leading to the precious Head of Marketing role, a title my parents could be excited about. They couldn't wait to tell everyone that their daughter was a success and no longer merely a junior marketing executive at the small publishing firm where I'd worked since leaving uni.

I wanted to make them proud, I really did. I'd already disappointed them with the Tim situation, so when this 'manager' job turned out to be more of an 'assistant' position I didn't have the heart to tell them. The truth was I spent my time running errands and reports for Sophie, the actual Head of Marketing, and I hated my life in Edinburgh. But instead, when I went home to visit them, I pretended my job and my life here was brilliant.

Mairi was the one person I could be honest with and I sent her occasional fake emails of my resignation.

"My life is over, *again*," I laughed. "I think I need an emergency round-the-world first-class-all-the-way trip-of-a-lifetime trip this time. But only if you're free?"

As a busy PA, Mairi's time was precious. I sensed her mentally scanning her desk diary. She let out a sigh.

"Five minutes. Pret, Hanover Street. You're buying."

Before I could thank her she'd already hung up.

I pocketed my phone and heaved my box of office paraphernalia in front of me like a shield against any more mess. Keeping my head as high as I could, I made my way to Hanover Street.

What. A. Morning.

How could this have happened? Half an hour ago I had a job, and one silly mistake later, here I was, unemployed.

In the future, my firing might be reduced to a funny anecdote, but right now replaying the horrifying moment the whole office accidentally received my email made me shudder.

Blissfully unaware (and still mopping up the coffee I'd spilt when Sophie barked an order that caused me to jump) I'd wondered why everyone was glaring in my direction. Everyone except Dave, of course — the Head of Finance's attention was still directed at his tablet and, I suspected, a fresh wave of cat videos. It started to sink in that something was not right when my inbox pinged with a new message from Phil, the Head of Operations.

Subject: SEE ME.

Beneath the single row of question marks in his email, I saw the message he was replying to. My throat went dry. Oh my god, oh my god.

I mean, they were definitely my words, but they weren't *really* my words, you know? These fantasy emails helped me get through the days, saying all the things I would never say out loud. What's that therapy where you go into another room and scream into a pillow? It was like that. Mairi says they are a waste of my writing degree, but I was stuck career-wise. There were a hundred different reasons this job was wrong for me, and I usually listed them in the email. But no one in this office was ever meant to read them.

No one. I wasn't being intentionally mean.

I took a deep breath. I looked at the doors. I wondered if I could make a run for it, pretend I was sick and head home.

Before I could move Julie from HR had come sauntering over, marshalled by Sophie and Nathan from accounts, looking even more harassed than usual.

"Please come with us," she said with the same firm voice in which she told everyone that, yes, they did have to work the English bank holidays.

I cringed inwardly, then stood up and followed the party of three into the glass box meeting room. What else could I do? I kept my head down but was aware of the eyes of everyone in the office staring at me. I couldn't blame them — I'd just betrayed them with my stupid email.

I'd mentioned that Dave is always watching cat videos — which isn't even a reason why I was in the wrong job, it just got on my wick. I'd also written that Nathan is creepy, that he lingers just *slightly* too long and *slightly* too close in the staff room when you're making coffee. And Maria. Oh, god — Maria is just sooo boring. Everyone thinks so, not just me! But it was me who wrote in such detail about how I don't care about her grandchildren, or her cats, or her plants, or... oh God, what had I done?

In the meeting room, Julie talked me through the many ways I could have handed in my resignation if I thought a career at JD Banff and Partners was not for me.

I kept my gaze downwards as she droned on. But all I could think about was poor Mum and Dad. Isn't that silly?

After dashing their hopes of no longer having Tim Hayward as a son-in-law, I was going to disappoint them further by never ever ever — like *ever* — becoming Head of Marketing at JD Banff and partners. These last few months had been hard on them. I'd seen the way they looked at each other when I visited, pretending that everything was fine. I knew they'd wanted to say something about the breakup but instead, they focussed on my wonderful job.

Maybe they'd already worked out that I was going to be a disappointment.

A flurry of movement outside the meeting room caused us all to turn our heads. The room was like a large square fish tank, and through the large glass windows, we could see that Campbell Maclean had entered the office.

Despite the situation I was in — we all knew I was about to be fired — my heart dared to skip a beat at the sight of Campbell, my office crush.

You see, the stuffy office atmosphere changed whenever Campbell was around. Everyone in the office liked Campbell Maclean. *Everyone.* Even though he was the son of the boss.

If this was a book, Campbell would be engaged to someone awful like Sophie. He'd be a hot but dense graduate drop-out, living off his daddy's chequebook, and she'd be trying to sell the company to his dad's enemies and decorating their new home in awful colours. But in real life, Campbell didn't like Sophie and had brought in a new customer management system that was saving the company thousands of pounds.

In real life, Campbell was not only ridiculously wealthy, but also clever, ambitious, and very 'easy on the eye', as my Nana would say. Meaning: hot, with a capital H-O-T.

And, if this *was* a book, he'd be the one who came in and saved me from this mess. He was the only person at JD Banff and Partners who'd ever spoken to me about anything other than JD Banff and Partners. We'd had occasional chats about TV shows and current affairs, and he was confident and happy and — did I mention he was hot?

Seeing him was the only thing that had brightened my day these last few months. Breaking up with Tim had been difficult, but Campbell made me hopeful. I could be attracted to someone. If I could be attracted to someone, then perhaps one day I might even meet someone. Maybe one day I would meet The One.

Not that it would be Campbell, I mean this wasn't a book. But he was nice to daydream about. Once, he'd stopped by my desk for a few minutes and admired my photo of Charlie, and I'd told him about my other life by the sea, and instead of going all quiet and awkward, he'd kept asking me questions. It was the only *real* conversation I'd ever had in that job.

Campbell was the only reason I still worked there.

He had this look, like he was looking right through me, I called it *The Look.* Then I knew he *saw* me. Mairi called it a spark, but I laughed it off. She was always hopeful for an office romance, but I knew Campbell and I would never fit together; we were from two different worlds. He had a key to the boardroom; I didn't even have the key to my desk drawer. He was in the same club that Sophie and half of the office were in — privately educated, wealthy, 'connected' to the 'right' people... They were always talking about ski seasons, summers in Italy, tennis matches, and their country homes. They lived in a different world to people like me — or maybe I lived in a different world from them.

Besides, he didn't even fancy me.

I stared at him now. Even Julie stopped waffling as we all watched Campbell as he was brought up to speed with my ridiculous act of career self-harm and why the whole office was watching us in the fish tank meeting room.

It was like watching a silent movie.

Someone showed him a computer screen and I watched his face as he read my email. Then my stomach dropped to the floor as I remembered what I had written...

"The only good part of my working day is when Campbell arrives and our eyes lock. He is easy on the eye, as my Nana would say."

Just as I was thinking that I really should stop listening to my Nana — or stop writing it down in emails, anyway — at that moment it looked like Campbell smiled.

Was it my imagination?

My heart skipped, hopeful that perhaps he returned the feeling. Did he think I — Isla with the shaggy copper hair and fringe that always got in her eyes — was also a babe?

As if sensing that *this* could be *our moment,* he looked up from the computer and stared directly at me.

Our eyes locked for a second. Then I looked away. I had no time for *The Look* today, this was serious.

I realised that I felt sorry for Campbell, and his dad — they were trying to run a good company. It wasn't their fault the staff slacked off and the office lacked a sense of community.

I'm not sure when Julie started speaking again, but I heard her tell me I had thirty minutes to pack up my things before I was escorted out of the building by Nathan.

"Sorry Isla," Nathan said as we stood at the door. "It's unfair, especially as half of what you said was true." He shrugged before walking away, leaving me outside the office building with my box of belongings.

Now I could add my career to the pile of mess that was my life.

And that was when I phoned Mairi.

2

I slid into a window seat at Pret to wait for Mairi and took a sip of water. It was important to remember the little things in times of crisis, and staying hydrated was one of them.

My mind raced to find some logical upside to being fired. I had a little bit of money saved for a rainy day, but with no job that wouldn't last long. I would have to budget. It may not seem like much of an upside, but I didn't mind budgeting. The constraint, the discipline… I secretly rather enjoyed it!

Tim had said it was one of the things he liked most about me, what he'd called my "budgeting skills". Which, when I thought about it, should have proved to be ominous about the state of our relationship. I'm pretty sure most guys like their girlfriend's butt in jeans, or their ability to look sexy in an old t-shirt. Mine had liked that I was *safe* and *dependable*. Until, of course, he didn't.

Ugh.

I sighed and stared out the window, watching the passersby, betting that they all had jobs they liked. I turned my thoughts to finding more positive outcomes — like, now I had a chance to find a job that I liked! One that not only paid the bills but gave me the freedom to use my imagination… And maybe be there for Charlie more than I had been.

Nana would have told me to go home and write my book because Nana was a hopeless romantic. Like me.

It was from my Nana I got my love of romantic movies, romance books, and the notion that one day I might write one of my own.

Nana had spearheaded my career as a best-selling author from the minute I could read. She'd been so proud when I graduated with my English literature degree and got my first job in the marketing department of a publishing firm.

"This is your big chance!" she'd said. She'd been so excited for me.

But transitioning from a marketing assistant to a best-selling author wasn't as easy as the romcoms I loved made it out to be. I never had time to write and when I did, I could never think of a good idea! So I threw myself into my job, and my relationship with Tim, and resigned myself to enjoy reading books instead of writing them.

Then, as the years went by, my life with Tim took centre stage, I didn't even have much time to read — I was prepping for my own romantic fairytale life of a big house by the sea, marriage, and babies. The holy trinity of fiction perfection! Until my life as I knew it came crashing down around me. I was devastated, all I had wanted since I was a little girl was to be married. A fairytale princess in a white dress.

Tim announced that the dream of marriage, babies and life by the sea was the last thing he wanted, least of all with me. My days as his girlfriend were numbered — which was ironic, considering my skills with numbers were one of the things he liked most about me.

Ahhh, Tim. The love of my life. My childhood sweetheart. Good, safe, average height, brown-haired, boxers not briefs, Tim-Never-Timothy. Tim, who made my Mum smile and my Dad laugh. Tim, who had sat me down in our beautiful flat to tell me that he thought we should go our separate ways.

I was so taken aback, I thought I'd misheard him. Was he talking about some new trendy immersive experience? Was 'Separate Ways' the new Edinburgh place to eat? Drink? Play? No. It turned out that 'separate ways' meant exactly that —separating our ways, along with our furniture, DVDs and lives. We were breaking up.

Finishing.

Finished.

Finito.

Done.

Undone.

Suddenly, my dreams of domestic bliss vanished.

Only — and I hate to admit this, because it's not very empowering, and while I'm a romantic, I'm also a modern woman, and I'll argue to anyone who will listen that you can be a modern empowered woman *and* a romantic — I was the most reluctant separator. I didn't want to be separated. Or single. I wanted to love and be loved.

I'd had everything I wanted, and then I didn't.

I still had Charlie, of course. Tim also gave up on *Charlie!* That hurt more than his discarding of me, but that was another thing altogether.

The man I had thought of as my one chance at happiness was gone and had left behind a box of DVDs that both of us knew he would never come back to collect. Because no one watches DVDs anymore.

No one. And now I had no job. My life was a clean slate.

I don't know how long I'd been sitting there, smiling out into the world passing by. Mairi's five minutes had stretched to nearer thirty, and before I knew it, I felt a little Nana optimism flooding through me.

Suddenly I realised I had exactly what I needed - time. Time to use however I wanted! Could this be a chance for me to do what my Nana had been telling me all these years and write my book, chapter and verse, from the first chapter to The End?

I slumped in my chair a little. It wouldn't be easy.

I still had no idea what to write about. And if I knew anything from working in publishing, to get anywhere close to a bestseller you needed a killer idea. Over the years ideas had come to me, and I'd scribbled them down, but were any of them good enough to get me a publishing deal?

Besides, how could I afford that kind of lifestyle? The rent on my flat was hefty, and that was before Charlie's dog walking fees, gas, electricity and food… Even *my* budgeting abilities couldn't see how I could make all that work.

But it was worth a try.

These were meant to be the best years of my life, and I'd been stuck on the hamster wheel of working to live. Perhaps this whole email catastrophe could be a blessing in disguise — perhaps, as well as job hunting, I could dedicate some time to researching an idea for my book. Maybe I should go home and spend some time with mum, dad and Nana, and see if inspiration would find me. The more I considered it, the more I was sure it would be the right thing.

Isn't that how it always happened in Hallmark movies?

I was shaken from my thoughts by a man on the street waving at me. My good manners propelled me to lift my hand to wave back, and in a flush of panic I registered that Campbell Maclean was not only waving at me, but he was also heading for the door of the coffee shop.

3

I didn't even hear what Campbell said as he pulled the chair out next to me and sat down — my brain was busy trying to compute what was happening.

Campbell Maclean was sitting next to me in a coffee shop! Campbell Maclean and Isla Barker were sitting together!

S.I.T.T.I.N.G like the childhood rhyme…

It felt like the stuff of fiction.

"Isla, sorry, I imagine your head must be all over the place," he said, signalling to the staff.

I nodded. Of course, he would know what effect he had on women, even though he didn't know that you went to the counter in Pret to order.

"They don't take your order, you have to go to the counter," I said, a little smirk on my face.

Rich people didn't understand the ways of us lowly people, queuing for our coffee.

"Sorry?" Campbell looked at me like *I* was the weirdo. "I was trying to notify them there's a spillage there." He pointed at a puddle on the floor. "Someone could fall over."

I stared at the spilt coffee and felt my face redden. Of course, Campbell would know about the real world! Campbell was *different*.

"Gosh, I'm sorry," I said. "That sounded ignorant of me — rich boy doesn't understand how coffee shops work… D'uh!"

I stole a glance at him and found him looking directly at me. His eyes were a luscious green, like precious gems, and framed by thick dark eyelashes. The emeralds glittered as he smiled, and my heart took a leap.

"I'll have you know, Isla Barker, I worked in a coffee shop all through uni. I make a mean cappuccino. Perfecting my latte art got me through some tough times."

He hung his head and smirked at me from beneath his mop of jet-black hair.

I stared at him with an open mouth. He'd used my full name in a sentence! This was unchartered territory for me. Campbell Maclean was not only devilishly handsome but had a sense of humour and knew how to converse with the common people. I wondered briefly if I had fallen and hit my head and was really in some emergency room, being treated for a concussion, daydreaming about this moment… Soon a doctor would shatter it all by peering into my eyes with a torch, saying, "She's fine, she'll live".

This couldn't be real.

"There you are!" Mairi swung into Pret, proving I wasn't daydreaming. I turned to her, a huge smile plastered on my face, hoping it was enough of a sign that I was out of my depth and needed help. I needed an emergency trip from my emergency trip!

Mairi had known me since junior school. She knew me inside and out. She would steer me gently away from Campbell and everything would be okay and I would never have to see him again.

Campbell had turned to look at Mairi.

"This is Campbell," I wittered, with the same stupid smile on my face, "He's my boss." Mairi stared from me to Campbell and back again.

"Boss's son, actually," Campbell corrected. He introduced himself and held out his hand for Mairi to shake.

Mairi flicked her eyes at me as she propelled her hand forward to shake Campbell's.

"Mairi Davenish," she said.

"You're Isla's childhood friend?" he said without missing a beat and as if it was the most common fact in the world.

My eyes widened — he'd remembered! During that one conversation we'd had I told him about Mairi, and he *remembered*!

Mairi smiled at him and nodded.

"We've known each other forever." She smiled and suddenly seemed like she was miles away.

Okay, this was bad: when Mairi spoke like she was on autopilot, I knew she needed help. I couldn't let her get stuck in the dazzling beam of Campbell Maclean's handsome headlights. The Look was just for me!

"And what do you do, Mairi?"

It was an easy enough question, but Mairi looked to me for answers I couldn't give.

"I - uh - work. Obviously. I work at Satchel and Proctor." Her smile had a hint of panic that she masked well. "I'm PA to the director," she added, ever the networker.

"You work with Giles Proctor?"

Mairi nodded and grinned like a lovestruck robot. "Yes! I'm his PA. Sorry, I already said that…"

"I know him well," Campbell said. "He's dad's squash buddy. Tell him I said hello. He's known me since I was knee-high to a grasshopper."

Campbell laughed, and Mairi and I joined in, and suddenly all three of us were laughing although I'm sure neither of us knew why. As the hilarity subsided I wriggled my eyebrows furiously in Mairi's direction, trying to send a message, but her attention was fixed on Campbell.

"Well," she said, "I'm just here to grab a coffee. Can't hang about — nice to meet you, Campbell. See you tonight?"

Campbell opened his mouth to answer, but I jumped in first.

"She means me," I said. "It's Halloween. We're going to a spooky salsa class."

"Sounds fun," Campbell said with a smile.

I worried he thought I meant salsa the dip, then Mairi gave a little salsa shake of her hips, turned on her heels and marched back out of the cafe.

I looked at Campbell and gave a weak smile.

"I thought she was here for coffee?" Campbell said, a quizzical look on his face.

"She's very busy. Her boss is quite important." I shrugged.

"Giles is a nice guy." Campbell nodded. "One of the good ones."

I nodded back. "Mairi likes working for him," I said, realising we'd entered a cul-de-sac of small talk.

For a moment neither of us said a word.

"Are you doing anything for Halloween?" I hate small talk.

Campbell looked at me and shook his head.

I had no idea how to speak to this man for any prolonged length of time. The last time we chatted, it had started when he'd seen the photo of Charlie on my desk and said "Cute dog". Charlie *was* cute and talking about Charlie was safe ground. I could talk to anyone about Charlie. But I was out of my depth here. There should be a rulebook for this kind of situation. *How to speak to rich people 101.* Perhaps that's the bestseller I should write?

Why wasn't Campbell talking? What did he want? Did he realise how awkward this was? Would he pick up on that and leave?

"I should get a coffee," he said, turning away from me and scanning the menu board. "Do you want one?"

No, I wanted to leave, to take my unemployed body home and curl up on my sofa and cuddle my dog, but I found myself nodding my head. I didn't want a coffee, but I also didn't want to appear rude.

"What can I get you? Latte, flat white? Normal milk, plant-based?" Campbell gave a slow smile as he questioned my coffee preference. Did he know how sexy he was? I could listen to him reel off coffee options for days.

"Isla?" He prompted me out of my reverie.

"An oat milk latte would be *ideal*," I said with a smile. Ideal? Who says that?!

I watched him as he went off to order — tall, broad-shouldered, confident… Then I caught a glimpse of myself in the mirrored end of the sandwich fridge and realised I was grinning inanely. My cheeks felt strange, I hadn't smiled so much in a long time. I looked at my reflection, the old happier version had crept back to replace the sad-looking girl that I usually saw.

My phone buzzed. A text from Mairi:

What is going on? Are you still there? Text me as soon as you leave!

I turned back to Campbell, who gave me a wave from the counter.

What *was* going on? I was as much in the dark as Mairi.

I sent her a reply:

?!?!?!?! followed by a smiley face emoji. That seemed to capture the mood.

Campbell placed two coffee cups on the counter, pushed one towards me, and then took a seat. I sat up straighter and looked at him expectantly, waiting for a clue as to why he was even here.

He took a sip of his coffee and nodded his approval.

"Good coffee," he said. I took a sip of mine and almost burnt my mouth, but still nodded in agreement.

What was going on? Was he going to ask me on a date? My mouth went dry and I felt like I might faint. I reached for my coffee cup, to have something to do with my hands.

"So, Isla," he said slowly, "sorry about this morning. My dad sent me after you."

My heart sank. There was nothing romantic going on at all. It was all business related. Then I realised that meant his dad knew what had happened... Ugh.

"We think you are a great asset to the company," he continued.

I'd been ridiculously stupid to think it was anything else and could only shake my head.

"I think we should forget that resignation email." He raised an eyebrow and smiled at me in his debonair Campbell way. "Although some parts of it we probably should discuss at some point?"

I cringed inwardly thinking of what I'd written, of what I'd written about *him*.

'He is a total babe...'

"Sorry, Campbell, it was unprofessional of me. It bordered on childish and immature."

"Some of it was interesting." Campbell took a sip of his coffee and looked me directly in the eye, I caught a brief glimpse of *The Look,* and then his business face was back on. He took a deep breath.

"Will you forget what happened this morning, put it down to an administrative error, and come back and work for us?"

He smiled, obviously expecting me to jump at the chance to go back to work for him and his dad and awful Sophie.

I hesitated. It was certainly flattering to be asked to come back. I'd been fired, and now they wanted me back! And I had walked out of the building with a mounting worry — how would I pay my rent? Would I ever find another job? What would my parents think?

But another feeling had washed over me when I left the office, too. A small part of me had felt something unexpected — relief. Opportunity. Possibility.

I shook my head slowly, not meeting Campbell's eyes.

"I don't think so," I said quietly, taking another sip of the scalding latte.

"What if we promoted you?"

Ahhh. So this was all business! He'd come armed with an agenda, and I ditched any idea I'd had that this was a chivalrous move or a romantic ambition.

"Oh no," I said, waving my hands in front of my mouth, trying to discreetly waft some air over my burnt tongue. "I wasn't trying to barter. Honestly," I reassured him. "I don't think it's the job for me."

It felt good to say it out loud.

It was true. I'd been stifled in the job, and felt like I'd been going backwards in my career. I wanted to explain that to Campbell.

"Being relegated to Sophie Cannon's assistant — " I began.

"Hold on," Campbell interrupted me, one perfect eyebrow on his perfect face raised. "Sophie's assistant? That's not why we hired you."

"Well, that's what she used me for. Getting coffee, dry-cleaning." I stared at my shoes.

Campbell's face turned serious. "Isla, I'm so sorry, I'll speak to — "

I cut him off. "It doesn't matter now. It gave me an insight into the company, and the financial sector is not where I see myself." The words started tumbling out and I shocked myself with my honesty. "I had hoped I'd be able to use my creativity. I should look for a role that nurtures that."

Campbell's eyes searched my face. I resisted the urge to reach out and smooth the stray hairs of his perfect fringe and put them back into place.

"Okay," he said, the word heavy with deliberation. "So, what if I were to hire you for a freelance project?"

I sat up a little straighter, I hadn't expected that.

"Doing what?"

"The same thing, marketing," he said, looking a little bit flustered. "Dad often has smaller things going on and I have a side project I'm hoping to set up. I'm looking to branch away from the business, I've been speaking about it with dad for a while now. You have experience in hospitality too, don't you?"

I nodded, secretly chuffed that Campbell was talking to me like a friend, not a colleague.

"I do. My parents own a small hotel."

"In the Borders, is that right? I've never been."

I nodded.

"Sea Colme Cottage. It's the best place on earth," I said and I meant it.

"Then I must come and see it," Campbell smiled. He took his phone out of his inside pocket and held it out to me. "Put your number in here, and I'll arrange a visit."

It felt strange to type my digits into his phone. I thought of all the phone numbers of all the girls he would have in there already. His contacts list would be full of serious dating prospects, not girls like me.

I saved my details and handed him back his phone. "Here you go. I won't be available for a few weeks, I'm going home for a bit."

He took a sip of his coffee and looked at me again.

"Do you have any plans while you're there?"

"I'm going to write a book," I said. Saying it out loud made it seem real, somehow. Also, very scary.

His face changed, and his small smile played on his lips.

"I can see you doing that, you have a…*way*… with words."

I cringed. "I'm sorry, no one was ever meant to read that email," I said, my face going red again as I thought of the words I'd written about Campbell. He looked down at his coffee cup, and I was thankful.

"I'm aiming to use my English Literature degree. It's worth a try. I have time now to follow my passion." I immediately felt a wave of heat in my cheeks saying the word passion sitting so close to Campbell.

"I liked what you wrote, it was…. insightful," Campbell said, his eyes finally meeting mine. I enjoyed the full glow of *The Look* for a whole 30 seconds before I pulled my eyes away from his.

"You're full of surprises, Isla Barker," he said softly. "I will miss seeing you in the office." He stood up. "I had better get back. I'll be in touch - about the project," he said, indicating his phone.

Then the strangest thing happened.

As he said goodbye, Campbell Maclean leaned forward and kissed me on the cheek as if it was the most natural thing in the world.

4

The views out of the train window were beautiful, I never tired of straining my neck to see them. It didn't matter what season we were in — spring, summer, winter, or late autumn like now — they all brought beauty. Although the journey from Edinburgh to North Berwick was short, it helped me transition from city girl to country girl. My home town, a bustling coastal town just beyond Edinburgh but feeling so different from it, was a great place to escape the mess that had become my city life.

My phone buzzed in my pocket. I knew it would be another text message from Mairi, even without looking. I was ignoring them because I had nothing to say. Yesterday's weird encounter with Campbell Maclean had sent my nerves through the roof and then crashing back down again, and now I was going home like the fool I felt.

"You're full of surprises, Isla Barker." He'd said. It made me feel exotic.

Why had he kissed me? I still didn't know.

I'd seen him kiss lots of people in the office before, that air-kissing hello thing people did. Was that all it was? It made me antsy. I kept touching my cheek, pretty sure I was irritating the area of skin with my fingers constantly running over it.

Not even Charlie's dark brown dog eyes could soothe me. My daydreaming was getting out of hand. It was just a kiss — why was I thinking it was something more?! Why on earth would the son of the boss, good-looking, charming, well-mannered, perfect Campbell Maclean consider me a romantic option? His appearance at the coffee shop had been purely an effort to get me to go back to work for the company, nothing more.

Surely.

Wasn't it?

I had gone straight home and texted Mairi to cancel the salsa class, poor Mairi was always trying to include me in her social life, but who needed spooky salsa? Instead, I retreated to the comfort of my sofa to cuddle with Charlie. We ordered some noodles and broccoli and re-watched *You've Got Mail* for the millionth time.

And we cried.

I know people will think dogs don't cry, but I wonder if they've ever had a dog like Charlie or watched a Tom Hanks and Meg Ryan movie.

He was in *bits*.

Some people also say dogs look like their owners, and everyone says I look like my mum — which is true, except for her hair which is poker straight, but I do secretly think I look a bit like Charlie. We both have shaggy copper hair that hangs over our brown eyes, and we are both considered 'happy-go-lucky' souls. We are both long-limbed and walk with purpose, although I don't often walk with my tongue hanging out. The similarities don't end there — we both love taking big walks up into the hills and on the beach, eating ice cream and curling up on the sofa crying at romantic films.

We're perfect for each other.

On Charlie's late-night walk around the block, I looked up at the moon, shining bright the way it always did, as if it hadn't a care in the world, and wondered what to do next. Although Campbell had promised me freelance work, he'd left the details vague. Technically I still had no job.

It made perfect sense to go home for a bit, where I could take long walks on the beach with Charlie and be among family. Being so close to the sea was like medicine for my soul. Like many who grew up in North Berwick, I was a beach baby. My parents ran a B&B right on the beach, so I'd grown up with sand between my toes and saltwater in my hair.

The B&B, Sea Colme Cottage, was a family affair and I'd spent my teenage summers and countless weekends helping them out. Even though the busy season had passed I was sure they'd appreciate an extra pair of hands around the place.

If it was summer, I'd have been able to pick up some instructor work from the local watersports centre, but it was out of season. With so many international visitors to the B&B, I'd seen a niche and taken instructor training in kayaking, paddle boarding, and leading wild swimming sessions. Although there would be a few tourists squeezing the last of the good weather out of the year, I doubted any would be going in the icy water.

My mind drifted back to summer. It was the best time to be in town. It was busy and bustling but we always felt part of it. Mum and dad had a monthly barbecue on the beach for everyone who lived nearby, a chance to get local people together and bond them to the landscape. They were a huge force for good in the local community — and that wasn't even the best bit. The highlight of every year was when mum organised North Berwick's Scandinavian Christmas Market.

Mum was obsessed with Scandi culture, and she'd been doing hygge long before it became Guardian-reader trendy. The Christmas Market was her passion, an annual drive to encourage the community to shop local and support small businesses. Every shop in the high street, and every small business in the surrounding area, had a stall at the market. North Berwick was like that, full of community — it was the biggest and best playground a child could wish for. There was nowhere like it.

Spending time with mum and dad would help take my mind off things, and I knew they'd fuss over Charlie. I felt like I hadn't even been doing that job well lately — Charlie deserved love, cuddles and fuss, and he loved playing on the beach. Going home would be good for both of us.

My phone rang. Mairi. Ugh.

I answered, glad that the reception would be patchy. I didn't want to talk about Campbell Maclean.

"Tell me everything you know about Campbell Maclean!" Her voice had an edge of excitement and for a brief second, my heart leapt. I *did* want to talk about Campbell Maclean! He was gorgeous, smart, funny, and — sigh — out of my league…

"I can't talk," I said, "the train is too busy."

Mairi sounded disappointed. "Are you going home?"

"Yes, mum and dad need a hand at the B&B. Plus all the fireworks displays in Edinburgh will be too much for Charlie." That was a lie. Charlie was an oddity of a dog who didn't mind fireworks.

"I knew I shouldn't have let you cancel Halloween salsa on me," said Mairi. I pictured her at her desk, typing furiously at some Very Important Spreadsheet.

I felt bad for having ignored her messages. She was my oldest friend and had been great at pulling me out of my slump after everything that happened with Tim-Never-Timothy. Ever the PA, she'd organised my diary so I'd be busy enough to not mope around with my bruised little heart. Mairi's parents lived a few streets away from mine, and we often took the train home on weekends together. But we hadn't been home together in a long time — her thriving work/social life gave her plenty of reasons to stay behind in Edinburgh.

"Was spooky salsa fun?"

"It was, everyone got very merry on the ghost punch. Lord knows what Giles put in it!" Mairi sounded cheerful, and too late I caught the change of tone as she shifted into Emergency Trip mode. "Right," she said. "I'm cancelling my Saturday morning pilates and catching the first train after work tonight."

"Oh Mairi, please! Don't cancel anything for me, honestly. I'm fine." I sounded as convincing as ever.

"I need to speak to mum and dad, plus the fireworks here will drive me mad," Mairi said. "And we need a catch-up — I want to hear all about you and Campbell Maclean."

"There's nothing to — "

"I'll see you at Barnacles!" she said and hung up before I could object.

We'd been going to Barnacles ever since we were allowed to wander off with our own money in our pocket. We used to think we were so sophisticated, ordering coffee at this tiny little cafe across from the public toilets, and sitting in the window so everyone could see us. How many hours had we spent there, over the years? Heads together, cackling over something or nothing — we'd gone there to get through the bad times and celebrate the good times. Barnacles was *our* place and Mairi was the sister I never had. As only children, we'd grown up sharing *everything*. We expected it from each other. And that degree of closeness meant I wasn't looking forward to her inquisition about Campbell. I didn't even have anything to tell her! He was the boss's son. He'd come to the cafe to ask me back to work. He was out of my league. End of story. I touched my cheek where he'd kissed me. *"You are full of surprises, Isla Barker."* His words echoed around my mind and I smiled, wishing it was the beginning of the story.

5

As we pulled into the station I gathered my things and followed Charlie to the train door. I'd walk the short distance to mum and dad's place. One of my favourite things about both North Berwick and Edinburgh was that they were such walkable places.

We walked along the platform, bag over my shoulder, both Charlie and I sniffing the air. The salty sea air smelled like home to me, the scent of my childhood. There was something so comforting about this town. When I was younger the fairytale was that I'd always live here, marry a local boy and have a house next door to mum and dads. Mairi would live around the corner and we'd go to Barnacles every day for coffee.

I had cried when I moved to Edinburgh permanently with Tim, he'd told me I would get used to it but I couldn't. I wasn't a city girl.

Charlie tugged on his lead, and I snapped out of my thoughts to give him some attention. The poor mutt had been a dumb witness to all my tears for the last few months. He pulled a little harder, which wasn't like him at all. I let him lead me, and looked up from the end of his nose to see what he was straining towards. There on the platform, just ahead of us, looking clean-shaven and handsome, was Tim.

Of course, he would be going home, it was the weekend! Tim and I used to do this journey together every week when we were a couple.

I caught my breath and tried to pull Charlie back, but he was determined to get to Tim, whining with excitement at such an unexpected reunion. My mind raced, and my first thought was to brush my hair out of my eyes. Whatever your hairdresser tells you, clarity of vision can be a girl's best friend. I hoisted my bag up on my shoulder and took a deep breath as Charlie pulled me forward.

"Hi, Tim," I said brightly as Charlie leapt up to lick his face.

Taken by surprise, Tim almost fell backwards with the force of Charlie's affection.

"Hello boy!" he said, ruffling a hand through his fur.

Tears welled in my eyes as I watched the two of them reunite. Then I remembered that Tim had given up on Charlie, and I pulled protectively on the lead, gently drawing Charlie back to me.

"He's so excited." I smiled. I could do this. I could have a normal conversation with the guy who broke my heart just six months ago…

Tim continued ruffling Charlie's fur and letting him lick his face until he calmed down. I took a treat out of my pocket to distract Charlie. He turned from Tim and sat wagging his tail, his mouth lolling open. He looked so stupidly happy.

I locked eyes with Tim, hoping he couldn't tell I was nervous.

"Are you down visiting?" Awkward small talk. Ugh.

"Mum and dad are having a party," he said, having the decency to look awkward too, brushing imaginary creases out of his shirt.

Tim smiled and I felt a blush creep up my neck and flood my cheeks. The crowd around thinned out as people left the station. Then I noticed the woman standing next to Tim. She was watching the two of us and smiling at Charlie.

A strange feeling started to build in my stomach. She lifted her gaze from the dog to me and gave me a huge smile, chewing gum as she grinned.

"Hi!" She waved.

Tim moved to stand beside her. "This is Chloe," he said with a sheepish look. "A friend from work."

Chloe was beachy blonde, with rows of perfect white teeth and green eyes. She looked like she belonged in an ad for surfboards, against a backdrop of Californian sunshine and rolling waves, not standing in the drizzle at North Berwick train station.

They looked at each other, and that's when I saw it: the secret look of lovers.

"And this," Tim said, ruffling Charlie's ears, "is Charlie!" It took me a moment to realise he was talking to Chloe, not me.

Chloe knelt down to rub Charlie's fur with the easy familiarity of a dog lover.

"Hello, you handsome boy! Well, aren't you gorgeous!" She let Charlie lick her face. And I let her let him. Ugh.

"I love dogs," she said. "I miss my two back home."

Chloe had abandoned her bags as she fussed over Charlie. Against my expectation, I had to admit I liked her instantly.

Tim gestured absently towards me. "Oh, and this is Isla."

Chloe looked up at me and smiled.

"Hi, Isla," she said with a small wave, wobbling as Charlie's enthusiasm threatened her crouching stability.

While Tim looked overjoyed to see Charlie, my mind raced to connect the dots. Tim's parent's party; Tim bringing his new girlfriend to meet them.

I stumbled backwards, instinctively pulling Charlie away.

"Nice to meet you, Chloe," I said. Sensing my desire for distance, Charlie came to sit beside me. I couldn't love him more at that moment.

I had to get away. I didn't trust myself with what I might do next. Laugh, cry, or scream. I knew I looked like a hot mess. It should be a law that you are not allowed to bump into your ex and his new girlfriend on days like this…

Tim looked somehow sad. "Hold on, Isla!" He leaned forward and whispered something to Chloe who nodded.

"Any chance we could spend some time with Charlie this weekend? Take him for a walk along the beach, maybe?" He leaned forward and tickled Charlie under the ears. "You'd like that wouldn't you boy?"

Charlie smiled and panted. Yes, Charlie really would like that! I, on the other hand, would not.

I stared from Tim to Chloe and back again, my mouth opening and closing as I worked out what to say. I had made it as easy as possible for Tim to continue seeing Charlie when he left me, but he'd politely refused, saying he didn't want to confuse him and that it was for the best. I still had the text messages as proof. Now he wanted to show off with him? No way — Charlie wasn't his dog now!

"I'll need to think about it," I said finally. I started to pull Charlie away. He resisted a little before trotting alongside me.

"Shall I message you?" Tim called after me. "To arrange?"

It was too much, so I picked up my pace. I didn't care if they thought badly of me. I wanted to be at mum and dad's, and I wanted Charlie all to myself.

6

I had eaten two scones already and was tucking into a third. Charlie was sitting in his basket on the floor chewing on a bone dad had brought from the butchers. Nana was reading a magazine and mum was peeling apples for crumble. The radio played in the background, and dad whistled as he carried out a DIY chore somewhere in the B&B.

I was home.

It was easy to forget my life's mess when I was sitting in the refuge of mum's kitchen. It was painted a burst of bright sunshine yellow and had been as much of a backdrop to my life as the beach outside.

With busy working parents, I'd sat at this kitchen table throughout my life — played here as a toddler, learned to eat from it, done my homework on it, moving from high-chair to stool to grown-up dining chair as the years passed. The kitchen was the hub of the house. It was where I'd peeled and chopped vegetables with mum and Nana for breakfast and dinner. I'd even daydreamed at this table with Mairi, many years ago, listening to Taylor Swift and wondering who we were going to end up with.

Now I was sitting at it, happily eating my body weight in baked goods, slathered with Nana's homemade jam.

"I never really liked Tim," Nana said out of nowhere, causing us all to look at her. Mum and I exchanged a quick glance then looked back at Nana. She hadn't looked up from her magazine.

"Didn't you?" Mum threw a look at Nana then raised her eyebrows at me before going back to peeling apples. "Well, it's no secret that I liked him," she sighed. She put down her peeling knife and reached out to pat my hand.

Mum hadn't just liked Tim, she'd *loved* him.

"He's good for you, Isla," she'd say with a misty look in her eyes. She'd remained hopeful that our breaking up was 'just a blip', one of those things young people needed to do before they realised everything was right there in front of them. I'd heard her telling dad when she thought I wasn't listening. She hoped I'd have the same fairytale teen romance that she'd had with dad. They'd met at school and dated since they were fifteen. But my mum and dad were made for each other in a way that Tim and I just weren't. It was obvious to anyone.

Like any self-respecting romantic, I'd used their relationship as the blueprint for mine and Tim's. But somehow he never seemed to be on the same page as me. For instance, he hadn't been overly tactile and had often winced when I launched myself at him with open arms. How could I achieve a 'happy ever after' with a man who didn't want hugs? As the months went by after we'd broken up, I could begin to admit to myself there had been cracks in our relationship, papered over with my hope and optimism. I wanted the same story as my parents. But I knew it was not to be. Not with Tim.

I hadn't yet told mum and dad the reason for my visit. As much as they didn't question me or push for answers, we didn't keep secrets in the Barker household.

"I saw Tim at the station, actually," I said through a mouthful of scone. My announcement stopped the activity in the kitchen. It seemed even the radio paused, waiting to find out more.

"You did?" mum said. She looked hopeful.

"He was with his new girlfriend." I had hoped to sound brighter than I felt, but it came out flat. I knew it would disappoint her.

Mum caught her breath and turned towards me. Nana put down her magazine and reached for my hand. I heard a clatter from somewhere upstairs that I could only imagine was dad reacting to the revelation.

"And," I said, feeling tears threatening, "he wants to spend time with Charlie."

I popped the last piece of jam-covered scone into my mouth, hoping it would stop tears from falling, but it didn't. A fat tear rolled from each eye, and I cried in the only way you can when you're with family.

Ugly.

I could just about bear the devastation Tim breaking up with me had caused my family, but I couldn't bear losing Charlie to him. Besides, he hadn't wanted him.

When we split he had coldly said I could keep him. And now he wanted him back? It had been hurtful when Tim, who had driven all the way to Lancaster with me to collect Charlie from a reputable breeder, had patiently trained him with me for a year, and laughed off his chewed-up designer shoes, our new sofa and collection of treasured comics — decided he wasn't a dog person after all and gave up all rights to Charlie.

Nana and mum moved to soothe me, my face a mixture of tears, snot, scone and jam.

I didn't mind the new girlfriend part, that was fine — it had been six months, a perfectly acceptable passage of time for him to find someone newer, better, blonder than me. But taking away my source of joy, Charlie, was unthinkable. I knew I wasn't okay with that. As if sensing it, Charlie came and lay his head on my knees, his huge brown eyes looking up at me, tail thudding on the kitchen floor.

Dad appeared in the kitchen doorway and surveyed the scene.

"Tim wants Charlie back," Nana said with a degree of scorn only older people can summon.

"No, Nana, he only wants to walk him," mum said. We all called Nana, Nana.

The apples were abandoned, and mum reached over and smoothed my wild hair. It had been a habit of hers since I was a child. However often my hair had been smoothed into ponytails and pleats, and as soon as it was released it sprung back to frizz.

"I've read about it in these magazines." Nana tapped the pile of magazines on the table. "It starts with a walk, then it'll be 'can we have him overnight?' then a holiday, then — " She clapped her hands, sitting back down at the table. "That's it, he's gone. Dog-napped from right under your nose."

Nana had always been one to focus on the cloud beyond the silver lining.

"Nana!" mum snapped. "Don't scare her like that. Tim is a nice boy, he wouldn't steal Charlie."

Dad moved around the table and hugged me.

"Tim's a good lad, Isla, he wouldn't do that. Besides — "

"No, Dave," Nana interrupted him. "He's got a new girlfriend. She saw them at the station." Nana ruffled Charlie's fur.

I looked over at dad, who looked suddenly like a man who had been given the worst news possible but didn't want to believe it just yet. I nodded glumly.

Dad had also been hopeful Tim and I would get back together. Our village was small and he played golf with Tim's dad.

"I'm sorry, love." Dad walked over to fill up the kettle, patting my shoulder as he went. "Life moves on. At least you have your career." He shot a look at mum to check he was saying the right thing, she smiled back.

I sighed and wiped my eyes with the back of my hand. Nana passed me a tissue and winked at me, picking up the local paper.

"Well, actually," I said, thinking I may as well unburden all my bad news at once. "I got fired."

I blew my nose into the tissue, avoiding eye contact with everyone in the kitchen. I couldn't even look at Charlie.

"Fired?" Mum, dad and Nana spoke as one. They had each frozen in their spots — dad had the kettle in his hand, mum held her apple knife poised, and Nana peered over the top of her newspaper.

I nodded.

"Well, technically I resigned." It was a technicality that offered no comfort. I stood up and walked to the kitchen bin, swinging the lid to throw my snotty tissue inside. "I'm sorry. I know I've let you all down, but I wasn't happy there."

My bravado couldn't hide the fact I felt awful.

My parents had been so proud of me for working at such a good firm. Such things mattered to them, and they told everyone who stayed at the B&B that their daughter was a marketing whizz with a top job in the city. Now, none of that was true.

7

"Well," Nana said, breaking the silence. "You never liked that job. Good riddance."

I was grateful to her for trying to lighten the situation, but the truth was etched in the expressions on my parent's faces. They looked at each other and said nothing. I had let them down.

"I'm so sorry," I said. "I know how much it means to you for me to do well — "

"Good riddance," said dad as mum leapt out of her seat.

"Finally!" she said, pulling me into a hug. "Oh Isla, we've been so worried about you. We knew it wasn't working. It's been awful seeing you struggle, love. Hasn't it, Dave?"

I was surprised to see my dad nodding.

"Awful," he said. "We could tell you weren't enjoying it. What with all those long hours and sky-high bills. We knew you only moved there to make Tim happy, and well, you don't have to make anyone happy but yourself anymore." Dad moved to place the kettle back in its stand and switched it on. Mum released me from her hug and we each took a seat. It was just like old times, all of us back around one table.

I was over the moon. I didn't know why I thought that they wouldn't have noticed. We were a close family.

"I'm thinking of staying for a bit, while I look for another job," I said carefully, I didn't want to impose on them.

"Oh, that's wonderful news, Isla!" Mum looked at dad whose face broke into a huge smile.

"It's better news than we could have hoped for," Dad cleared his throat. "Your mum and I have been wanting a little break to celebrate our anniversary and we had been wondering who might help out. Maybe — " He looked across at mum.

"Perhaps you could run things here for us?" Mum said in a rush, finishing dad's question for him. "It wouldn't be too much trouble. Would it?"

I looked at my parents. I could burst with love for them both. They worked so hard and deserved a break. I couldn't remember when they hadn't been in this kitchen or this B&B.

"Nana will help, of course, and we'll ask Loretta to do some extra hours." Mum's voice was cautious.

"What do you think?" Dad reached out and entwined his fingers with mums.

I felt a weight lift from my shoulders. They wanted me back home.

"There's a cruise up the Norwegian fjords we have always wanted to do," Dad said. "They guarantee you'll see the Northern Lights!"

I knew they'd always wanted to see the Northern Lights. Even *I* wanted them to see the Northern Lights.

"It's four weeks and takes us all around Finland, Denmark, and Norway," mum said, sounding excited just at the idea of it. Her face glowed. I hadn't seen them both this excited in years. "It's all a bit last-minute but it's the best time to go before we get busy with Christmas. Don't worry, our new booking system deals with everything for the business — taking payments, storing emails, everything. We can set it to take limited bookings, so you won't be overrun with any last-minute guests…"

She stopped to catch her breath and looked up at Dad, who stood up from the table and moved behind mum to squeeze her shoulders. They both looked at me.

"It should be manageable, Isla," dad said. "If you think you could do it?"

I stared at their hopeful faces and realised I hadn't spoken.

"Of course!" I exclaimed, clapping my hands together, full of excitement for them both. "This is wonderful! I'd love to help out. You must go! Nana and I can handle things here."

I looked at Nana for confirmation, who nodded.

"I told you Isla would help out." She laughed and picked up her newspaper. "These two have been too frightened to ask you," she said, turning to me. "But Nana knew." She tapped her nose. "Nana knew it would all work out. Just like I knew Tim wasn't 'the One. The One is still out there." Nana tapped her nose and winked at me. "I'll know him the minute I see him."

I winked back. I hoped she was right.

Soon, the air in the kitchen was crackling with energy as mum and dad talked over each other, describing the cruise, and the places they'd wanted to visit for years. Even Charlie barked enthusiastically, joining in with the excitement of the moment. Mum pulled out her laptop and showed me the itinerary, pointing out all of the cities they would disembark and stay in. They were going to do a week on either side in Norway and Denmark.

With a few clicks — and a small drama with dad's credit card — they were booked on their dream holiday. I wished it was as easy as that to make my wishes a reality.

Caught up in the moment, dad decided a Barker family celebration was needed. Mum suggested we go to Luciano's for dinner. It was the local Italian and the place we celebrated every family occasion, like most residents in town. Lucio and Maria were close friends of mum and dad.

I left them chattering in the kitchen and took Charlie across to the beach for a pre-dinner walk, trying to let everything sink in. The November air was fresh, you could feel winter on its heels. I threw a stick into the sand ahead of us, and as Charlie raced off to catch it I felt a renewed sense of something I hadn't felt in a long time.

Hope.

Things had fallen into place like autumn leaves falling to the ground.

Time at home would give me time to figure out what I should do next. A whole month at home would be just the tonic I needed. I'd watched mum and dad running the B&B for years, and knew every bit of the business almost as well as they did.

What could possibly go wrong?

8

Mairi and I sat at our favourite table in Barnacles, a plate of sweet potato fries and calamari in front of us.

"I can't believe they're finally doing it," Mairi said, scooping a dollop of mayo onto her fry and shovelling it into her mouth. "Your parents have been talking about that trip ever since I've known them." She covered her mouth while she spoke.

I nodded and chewed a calamari ring.

Mum had a photo of the Northern Lights pinned to the fridge, it had been there for years. Whenever we had Scandinavian guests staying with us, mum grilled them for information on their country, food, language, then culture. Scandinavian culture fascinated her. She was always sending me hygge quotes, and our house was decorated with candles, blankets, and pillows. Dad often made a joke there was no room for any of us, but we all loved the cosiness she had created.

"I know. I'm so happy she's finally getting to tick it off her bucket list." I swallowed my mouthful of calamari.

"But enough about them," Mairi said, pointing a sweet potato fry in my direction. "You still need to give me details on the handsome boss's son."

I shook my head. "There's nothing to tell." I shrugged. It was true. "He asked me to come back to work, and I said no thank you. Then he offered me some freelance work." I didn't tell her about the kiss, she'd only think it meant something.

I picked up another calamari ring to dip into the garlicky aioli.

Mairi tipped her head to one side and looked at me.

"I know you," she said. "There's more to this."

I shook my head. "I swear there isn't. He's the boss's son and I'm — " I looked around Barnacle with affection. "I'm here…"

Barnacle was a busy local bar, but its owners, Hetty and Burt, were getting on and we all knew they were longing to retire.

I don't think the interior had been decorated in all the years I had been living here. But it was clean and served the best food. Barnacles wasn't a place for Tripadvisors or Facebook check-ins, and as locals, we were so glad for a place that was ours. Yes, we liked summer visitors to enjoy our town, but when they packed up and left, it was our home. We were proud of it.

Besides, Barnacles couldn't always cope with the volume of summer visitors, and sometimes people left bad reviews online. It was so unfair, Hetty and Burt worked hard and the cafe didn't even have a website! They had the business up for sale as a going concern, but hadn't been impressed with any of the potential buyers so were still running it.

"So," Mairi said, wiping her hands on a napkin. "How do you think you'll manage with the B&B?"

It was a fair question and one that I hadn't put too much thought into. Mum and dad seemed to think I could do it, so I had confidence in them. Mum had left an extensive to-do list and an old Filofax of numbers in case of emergency. She'd changed the booking system to run on the half capacity of guests — November was the quietest time of the year, so there shouldn't be too much to trouble me.

"Mum said the place should run itself, she has a super-duper new booking system, it takes care of everything." I smiled. I'd helped out every summer since I could walk, and besides, I wouldn't have to do any admin, as they'd take care of that when they returned.

Nana would be around too, of course. Mum had asked me to look after her, without Nana knowing of course. If Nana caught one whiff of mum asking me to look after her, she wouldn't be happy.

"The only thing that is bothering me is the Christmas Market. Mum wants me to take on the organisation of it this year."

I toyed with my napkin.

"You're organising the Christmas Market?" Mairi had picked up a sweet potato fry and now held it midway to her mouth, eyes wide.

I nodded.

"Well, not quite, more overseeing, mum says the organisation is mostly done. I will keep an eye on emails for late stallholder applications."

The annual Christmas market was in its fifth year. It was held on the beach opposite Sea Colme Cottage. For me, it signalled the start of the festive season. Shopkeepers from the town took pop-up stalls with a Christmas theme. Dad ran a food stall, stocked with turkey burgers, bacon and sausages, and speakers played Christmas carols. There were wreath-making workshops and the wool shop held a knitting circle for charity, there was a prize for the best scones and decorated Christmas cake.

It had a great community spirit, but organising it took Mum months of preparation — I was worried it would be too much of a responsibility for me.

But mum assured me that most of the organisation was taken care of — the real work happened on the weekend of the event, which they'd be back in time for.

I loved the market and wanted to make Mum proud, it was her special gift to the community and over the years it had grown into quite the event.

And for me, the real magic happened *after* the market. Once everything was tidied away, Nana brought a huge basin of her famous boozy eggnog, and dad created a fire pit on the beach. Then, we got all wrapped up against the chill and ate leftovers and sang Christmas songs and carols. It was a time to give thanks for the year that passed and focus on the year ahead. Everyone was invited, and they brought their own picnic blankets and treats. The stars always shone brightly and it was my favourite time of the winter. Like that first watching of Tim Burton's *A Nightmare Before Christmas*, it signalled the start of the holiday season.

This year, mum would be experiencing real Christmas markets in Norway and had passed the baton over to me. It was a daunting task.

"You'll help me won't you?" I asked Mairi, who pursed her lips and turned her head to the side.

"I'll try but you know how busy I get at the end of the year." She shrugged. "Anyway, you might be getting some help from the big boss man's son." She giggled.

"Why do you keep saying that?" I laughed along with her.

"I saw something between the two of you, I guess," she said. Then her face took on a serious look. "Besides, it's nice to have a crush, isn't it? Tim has moved on. Although I can't believe he'd bring his new girlfriend here so soon..." Mairi shook her head.

I knew she was protecting me, but Tim had wanted to move on, he was doing exactly what he said he wanted to do.

"It has been six months." I picked at the fries. Six long months.

We sat in silence for a few minutes.

"What was it like seeing him?" Mairi asked gently.

I shrugged.

"Okay, I guess."

I didn't trust myself to say anything more, and Mairi knew me well enough not to press further.

"Will you let him look after Charlie? You're going to be busy."

I didn't need reminding. The thought of dealing with the B&B, the market organisation, trying to write *something*, the freelance work from JD Banff and Partners, as well as Charlie, was niggling away at the back of my mind.

"He'll need a daily walk if he is going to hang around the B&B all day," I said. "I can't rely on Nana, he'd pull her over if she tried to walk him."

I slumped in my chair. I was fiercely protective of Charlie, and anyway, Tim hadn't wanted him!

"Do you remember Sky McKay from school? Mum said she's opened a dog-walking business, maybe you could ask her? Here, look." Mairi had scrolled on her phone to Sky's facebook page, Sky's the LiMutts. Dog-walking businesses were always named so inventively.

"I'll have a think, although I won't have the spare cash for a dog walker." I shrugged. I had to plan carefully, a dog walker would be a luxury at the moment. His walker in Edinburgh had charged a small fortune which had been fine on Edinburgh wages.

"Well, I agree he can't just swoop back in now and pretend the last six months hadn't happened. But — " Mairi hesitated, a trait that was unlike her. "You might need him. Especially if you are going to try to find time to write. You need to move on."

"I know." I picked up the last sweet potato fry and popped it into my mouth. I didn't need to be told.

"Do you have an idea yet?" Mairi asked, swiftly changing the subject.

"I do." I smiled.

"Are you ready to tell me?" Mairi asked.

I nodded. Confidence in my idea grew every day.

"I was thinking about writing about here," I said, waving my hand in a circle. "With a fiction angle, of course, taking inspiration from the sea life, the birds."

I was happy with the idea of honouring North Berwick in this way, it's an idea I'd toyed with on and off for years. Now felt like the right time.

"What?" I saw something in Mairi's face, a flicker of — doubt.

"Nothing," she said, brushing me off. "It's just, is there enough to write about here?"

I was a little taken aback.

"Of course," I laughed. "Lots!"

Mairi's look said she disagreed, and that made me laugh more.

"You are funny, Mairi. Lots goes on here. I'll settle up" I picked up my coat and went to the counter to pay.

I hoped the Charlie situation would resolve itself and we'd get into a routine. He'd been used to staying at home while I worked. His dog walker came in at 10 am and he was back at home by 12 to snooze until I got in from work at 5:30 pm. I'd start by setting my alarm early and walking him on the beach first thing in the morning, which should settle him for the morning and I'd try to walk him in the afternoon before I sat down to write. With any luck, I should be able to write between guest check-in and check-outs.

We waved to Burt and Hetty as we left. Outside, Mairi linked arms with me.

"I love it here, don't you?" I said, looking up at the starry sky.

Mairi rested her head on my shoulder and murmured her agreement.

"Do you think we'll both live here when we're older?" I asked. I liked to think Mairi and I really would live here forever.

"We are older!" Mairi answered, pulling her coat tighter with a shiver. "Brrrr. it's starting to get quite cold now, I need warmer climates!"

"We'll probably have to be spinsters with cats." I was warming up to the possibility of having all of my loved ones living close by.

"What other choice will we have? No cute guys ever come to North Berwick!" Mairi laughed.

"Luckily, it's very on-trend to be a dog or cat lady," I said.

I was mentally preparing myself for a solo life with dogs, I had Charlie and that was everything. Mairi patted my arm.

"I'm sure things will change. They always do." She was unusually optimistic.

We walked to the end of the road, where she was to turn one way and I would go the other. I remembered how, when we were younger, we'd wave at each other until we were completely out of sight. This street was full of the echoes of our childhood, and I adored it.

As I walked the rest of the way alone, my thoughts returned to comfort and happiness. Something deep in me wanted to move back here, to leave Edinburgh and return to the cosy comforts and familiarity of my home town.

If Mairi moved back too we could start living the life we had dreamed of as kids, and not just talk about it! But one of us had to make the move first.

I had a month to prove that it could work for me and Charlie, and then convince Mairi that she should move back too.

9

Waking up at home always gave me a feeling of contentment. I was surrounded by the familiar smells of the bed and breakfast, the lingering smell of mum and Nana's baking, mum's assortment of candles, the sunlight streaming through the south-facing windows of my bedroom, and the warmth of Charlie nestled on my feet.

So much had happened since I returned, had it only been a week?

Mum and dad had left on their trip of a lifetime with hugs and waves goodbye and Nana and I were now officially in charge of Sea Colme Cottage. Things were going well, the new booking system was a dream, it was exactly as mum had said — easily manageable!

I stretched in the bed, careful not to move Charlie too much and enjoying that brief moment of relaxation before he sprung into life.

I loved sleeping in this room, my childhood bedroom. Mum had given it a hygge once-over after I moved to Edinburgh. Gone were my teenage posters of Taylor Swift, and Justin Beiber and tie-dye bedding, now it was sophisticated with muted greys and silvers, candles in glass hurricane holders, throw pillows and artwork of the beach in silky tones on the walls.

I had a desk under the window. It faced the beach, and I credited that view with helping me make good progress with my writing. I'd mapped out a story and was working on breaking down the chapters before beginning to expand on them.

I sat up gingerly and stretched my arms above my head, feeling the sleepiness fall away. I moved to my desk to look over my notes for the day ahead, and pulled the blinds up, flooding the room with golden-yellow sunlight.

I could see an assortment of dog walkers already trekking the sandy beach, throwing sticks and gathering to exchange the ritual morning's small talk. I dressed quickly, Charlie watching me lazily from the bed, his tail thumping. I knew as soon as I said the W-word he'd bounce up, so I dressed with as much care as I could.

I could hear the staff downstairs, getting breakfast ready for the guests. Nana's laugh travelled up to the second floor and made me smile. I was happier than I thought I could be.

"Ready for a walk, Charlie?" I whispered and he cocked his head up, thumped his tail and then sprang at me from the bed. I cuddled him and ruffled his fur, already laughing. We clattered downstairs and I hooked him up to his lead, we had 30 minutes before I was due in the kitchen.

The outside air was fresh and he strained to get to the beach and play with the other cavorting canines. Once we were safely over the road and far enough away from the traffic I released him and watched as he ran into the distance.

While Charlie loved the park close to where we lived in town, he was a beach dog at heart. Tim and I had spent his early months here, playing on the beach, me daydreaming of the day we'd have a family to play alongside Charlie.

I straightened my fleece as a cold gust of air got under it. Well, it was just me and Charlie now, the two of us against the world. Tim had moved on and Mairi was right — I should, too.

My thoughts drifted to Campbell.

What would it be like to date someone like Campbell Maclean? My thoughts flew in eight different directions at once, imagining all the things a man like that would bring to my life.

I instinctively touched my hair, piled loosely in its usual riot of frizz and curl. I would probably have to get something done about that if I was to date someone like Campbell.

"Is that your bloody dog?"

I snapped myself out of my thoughts and looked for Charlie, my eyes scanning the beach in a panic. He was playing at the edge of the waves with a smaller dog. I relaxed, he was fine.

"He's playing," I said, turning to find the person who had spoken.

"He won't leave my dog alone!"

A tall guy with a beanie hat was walking towards me. The hat was pulled low on his head and he wore an orange gilet and skinny jeans. He looked like he'd just stepped out of a Hollister advert.

"He's just playing," I said, trying to sound reassuring. "He's a big softie!" I offered a smile. Charlie was a big dog but he was harmless.

"Pickles!" The guy shouted. *"Pickles!"*

We both watched the dogs playing together in the waves, happily ignoring us, caught up with playtime.

"Charlie!" I joined in, knowing full well Charlie wouldn't listen to me. "He's still a pup," I said to the guy. Making excuses for Charlie's tardy behaviour came naturally to me.

"Pickles likes to play," the guy said, relaxing a little. "She has selective hearing too."

He moved his hat a little further up his head revealing a thick blonde fringe. Then he gave a slow smile and I felt like the sun had streamed along the beach as his face lit up. It was early morning and there was no other excuse for the heat I felt in my cheeks. I felt his eyes studying me, my hair, my tatty jeans, catching his eyes flicking up and down.

If we were dogs we would have gone straight in and sniffed each other's butts.

"I'm glad they're having fun," I said as we fell into a natural step alongside each other, drifting towards our dogs.

"Me too," he added. I caught the whiff of an accent. He must be a holidaymaker.

"I'm Isla. Charlie and I live over there," I said, pointing back over at Sea Colme. "He's used to this beach."

"I'm Johnny." He lifted his hand up in a half-wave, half-salute. "We live that way." He gestured towards the other end of the beach, past the golf courses.

"I wondered if you were a holidaymaker," I confessed. "We haven't seen you before?"

I always enjoy chatting with other dog walkers. You get a unique insight into their lives without ever truly knowing them. And they always know, without you telling them, how much you love your dog.

"I moved here during the pandemic," Johnny said, sounding slightly aggrieved at life. "I work from home, and it seemed like a good place to work."

He didn't need to convince me of that!

"How's it working out for you?"

He nodded hesitantly. "Good, I love being by the sea."

I waited for a 'but', which didn't come.

"Me too," I said. "I grew up here, so if you ever need a tour guide, pop by and say hello. I'm here for the month."

I stopped myself before I said anything else. I'd crossed the dog walkers' small talk boundary, and could see Johnny thinking I'd overstepped a line. I always spoke too much!

Johnny looked sideways at me and back over at the B&B.

"Thanks, it's good to have friends in the area — "

At that moment a soaking-wet Charlie jumped up at him, knocking him off balance, and licking his face.

I reached forward to grab hold of Charlie and at that moment Pickles barrelled through between my feet... I lost my footing, and as I scrambled to save myself from falling and push Charlie out of the way, I felt Johnny reach for my hands to help. Too late!

It was straight out of a movie.

I could feel myself falling, and not just because of gravity and a lack of balance. I saw a hint of a smile on Johnny's face, and my heart leapt the tiniest bit. I landed on top of him in the sand, the dogs scampering around us as our hands entwined above Johnny's head.

For a split second, we stared at each other, our faces inches apart. He had freckles on the top of his nose. His breath smelled of morning coffee. His eyes were like whirls of caramel, glints of orange and flecks of amber. I was transfixed until I felt a rush of guilt about being so intimate with a total stranger.

"Sorry!"

We both moved into apologetic recovery mode. I untangled my hands and rolled off Johnny's chest, and lay on my back staring at the sky. Charlie had run back to the waves with Pickles, like they hadn't just caused a mini catastrophe...

"That's some dog you have there..." Johnny was sitting rubbing his head.

My watch bleeped with the alarm I'd set. Dog walking time was over, and I had to get back to the B&B to work, but I was going to be late, especially as I needed to change out of these sandy wet clothes.

I hauled myself up and dusted off as much sand as I could.

"I'm sorry, I need to go, the breakfast shift starts soon."

Johnnie reached for his beanie, which had dislodged during our collision. He sat on the sand, looking dazed.

This was my moment to make a move or… or miss the opportunity.

"Do you want to come over?" I said, gesturing back to the house. "I could get you a coffee, to say sorry?"

Johnny slowly got to his feet.

"It's okay, I need to log on at work." He dusted the sand from his jeans. Pickles came running over, a gorgeous barrel of a French Bulldog with a pink collar. Johnny hooked the lead to her collar. As Charlie trotted behind her I managed to grab his collar and leash him, too.

"Well," I said, my face flushed. "It was nice to meet you."

Johnny gave a small nod and patted Charlie.

"Eventful morning!" he said cheerfully. Then he turned and walked away.

I stared after him for a few moments. Hadn't Mairi said no cute guys came to North Berwick?!

As I walked back to Sea Colme Cottage with Charlie, I texted her.

"You'll never guess what just happened! I had a meet cute straight out of a movie! On the beach!"

If she believed these things happened, maybe my plan would work out after all.

10

Sea Colme Cottage had built a reputation for providing a great location, a good night's sleep, a home-cooked breakfast and afternoon tea. To uphold that level of expectation among guests while mum and dad were away, the plan was that Nana would take the morning breakfast cooking shift and I'd serve up the afternoon tea, both of us helped by Loretta.

A full Scottish breakfast of sausages, bacon, eggs, black pudding, potato scones and mushrooms was offered, and guests rarely refused it. Porridge and granola were also offered, alongside fruit platters. Breakfast wasn't a rushed affair and mum had decorated the dining room in blues and greys so guests felt relaxed simply by being there, lingering over breakfast, planning their day, and rarely refusing a second cup of tea or coffee.

I kept an eye on Nana in the kitchen, just to be sure she was okay and cooking the breakfast wasn't too much to handle. Watching her flip the fried eggs it seemed to me that mum had nothing to worry about — although Nana was in her seventies she could give us all a run for our money!

We had three rooms booked — a couple from Glasgow staying in the family room with their baby; a cyclist was in the single room, keeping herself to herself; and a retired couple, both teachers on holiday from York, were staying in the attic room at the back.

That room had the best view in the whole town, dad said. It looked up at Berwick Law, an extinct volcanic peak that offered a hearty climb for the more energetic guests. I joked with the teachers about a walk after breakfast but they insisted they were here to relax and unwind and were keen to go to the Sea Bird centre and try to spot some puffins and seals. I gave them a few tips for best spotting sights and reminded them we served afternoon tea at three o'clock every day. Mum's apple and cinnamon scones were famous on Tripadvisor, though it was Nana's secret recipe.

I did a brief check of the bookings, noting that the family were checking out today and we were due a new guest, Mrs Paton — I recognised the name, she was one of mum and dad's regulars. She had been coming every year since I was a kid. Her requested room was ready and waiting, all I had to do was open the window to air it, as I knew she liked.

At the end of the breakfast service, I was kept busy enough with clearing plates that I didn't get a chance to think about my close encounter with Johnny earlier that morning. It was only when I went into the kitchen to get a belated cup of coffee that the incident crept back into my mind.

Nana was putting the breakfast leftovers on the table, ready for the staff to have breakfast after the guests had left for the day. She slipped some sausages into Charlie's bowl too, so he wasn't left out.

"Nana, you'll never guess what happened to me earlier."

She looked at me with a frown, always expecting the worst. "Go on," she said, wiping her hands on her apron and moving to fill her cup from a teapot. Mum's kitchen always had a pot of tea on the go, it was a Barker family tradition. When I grew up and it became apparent I wouldn't drink the stuff, mum had joked that she should get me a DNA test. All Barker women drink copious amounts of tea, but I'd just never got the taste for it. I preferred herbal teas and coffee.

"I was walking Charlie on the beach and literally *fell* onto a guy."

I knew Nana loved this kind of story. She cackled with laughter.

"How on earth did you manage that?"

We both took well-deserved seats at the table and I told her the whole story, slightly embellishing the romantic overtones for her benefit.

Nana was a permanent fixture in our house and although she was tiny, she ruled the roost. Despite standing just five feet high in her stockings, and despite being as thin as a rake, Nana Barker was a powerhouse. A halo of fluffy grey hair framed her face, and she smelled permanently of lemon cologne.

Although grandpa had died when I was a baby, I felt as if I knew him — Nana told me countless stories of him and their life together. They'd only had one child, and had been over the moon when she'd married my dad and their family grew. Grandpa was so delighted when I was born, that he bought a round of drinks for everyone at the local pub!

He'd been a fisherman, and his family were North Berwick royalty, going back generations. Their story was so romantic. Nana had met him on a family holiday one summer. They'd become pen pals for a year, then one day, grandpa appeared at her family home in Edinburgh and asked for permission to marry her. Nana said she and her sisters had hidden at the windows, watching him approach the house, looking so handsome in his smart suit. The B&B was littered with photos of him, and my favourite was one of him fixing fishing lines at the harbour, a pipe in his mouth. He was smiling into the camera. Nana had taken the photo, his huge smile had been for her. One thing that struck me when I was packing up my flat after the debacle with Tim, was that none of the photos I had taken of him had that same smile. That smile of pure love.

"Do you think you'll see him again?" Nana asked, reaching for a biscuit.

I took one too and dunked it in my coffee cup.

"I guess," I said, playing it casually as I crunched the biscuit. "He says he lives here."

"Ooh, I wonder if he's 'The One!" She winked and flashed her mischievous smile.

Nana was worse than Mairi when it came to me dating and finding 'The One' but I indulged her. At least she wouldn't sign me up for salsa classes, she'd just pop on one of our favourite movies, or knit me a new scarf.

Loretta joined us at the table, filling her plate with breakfast items and fresh tea. She'd been with us for years and was considered family.

"Did you hear?" Nana said to her. "Isla fell head over heels for a guy on the beach this morning. Over *his* heels, I mean!"

She chuckled as Loretta turned to me, waiting for me to elaborate. I filled her in on the details.

"Did he wear an orange lifesaver?" Loretta asked, and I nodded, wary as to why she would pick up on that detail.

"He's my neighbour, nice guy. Johnny, right? That dog is so cute." She looked across to Charlie's where he was snoozing, "Sorry Charlie, not as cute as you!"

Charlie looked up from his basket in the corner and barked. We all laughed.

"Tell us all about him, Lo," Nana said, pushing Loretta for details.

Loretta shook her head. "I don't know much," she said, though I suspected she knew more than she would be willing to admit. "He moved here with a girl, not long after the start of lockdown."

"They call her 'neighbourhood watch'," Nana said, nudging me and giving a wink.

Loretta blushed. "I wasn't being nosy! There was nothing else happening back then, remember? You couldn't help but notice everything, every person in the street."

We all nodded. I remembered how it felt strange and exotic at the time — being confined to our houses, with nothing to do but look out at the world from behind our windows.

"Well," Loretta said, looking at me and raising an eyebrow. "She moved out a few months ago. I haven't seen her since."

Nana caught my eye and we oohed and giggled together at this bit of gossip. It felt good to have some light relief after the heaviness of the last months.

"Relationships are not easy," Loretta said. "Take my Pete — he's a good man, but over lockdown, he drove me mad! How we stayed together is a miracle."

We understood the Lorette and Pete situation. We'd heard all about it before, as Loretta usually spoke about her husband in between work shifts. Seeing them together it was clear they adored each other, but Loretta needed to let off steam from time to time. Some days she could rant about him for ages, and some days she smiled wistfully, happy with her lot.

"Lockdown was difficult for lots of relationships," Nana said, bringing the conversation back to Johnny. "People weren't used to being forced to be together, whether they liked it or not. Perhaps that's what happened to your man and his lassie?"

Perhaps. I wouldn't allow myself to think about the possibility, not yet.

"Talking of your men. Did you read the email from Campbell?" Loretta wiped imaginary crumbs from the table.

It was an innocent enough question but I felt a prickle of sweat break out on my brow.

"My men?" I said, looking at Nana who immediately looked away.

"Nana!" I exclaimed. Nana had told the whole story to Loretta. "He's not my man," I said pointedly to Nana and then turned to Loretta, "Loretta, he's not my man." I shook my head. Of course, I'd like him to be, but that was beside the point.

"Hold on," I said, my mind whirring to life. "Did you say an email from Campbell?" I stammered with an effort of trying to sound casual.

Loretta sipped her tea and nodded. "I left it in the inbox, something about a visit."

Blood rushed to my cheeks, something not missed by Nana, who nudged Loretta to make sure she'd seen my discomfort too.

"Campbell... he emailed?" Words were giving up on me all of a sudden.

Loretta put her cup of tea down. "On Monday, I marked it for the personal folder," she said, apologetically. "Sorry, I thought you were checking the personal folder?"

They both stared at me, these two women, waiting for an explanation. I hadn't checked the personal folder, thinking I did not need to — no one would be personally contacting me at that email address. Would they?

"Is that *the* Campbell?" Nana asked, excitement in her voice.

I stared at mum's laptop and swallowed. "I think so unless we have a supplier called Campbell?" I looked at each of them in turn, looking for a way out.

Both shook their heads.

Ugh.

I reached for the laptop and held my breath while it booted up. Being old it took its time. Finally, I managed to open the inbox and scrolled to Campbell's email.

"Oh my God," I said, my hands flying to cover my mouth. I looked up at everyone. "He's coming here!"

Loretta gasped.

"When?" Nana asked.

I looked over at the clock on the kitchen wall.

"Today," I groaned. "It says he'll be here around eleven."

"That's in just over an hour!" Nana exclaimed.

I felt panic rising as I digested the enormity of my ex-bosses son coming to visit me, in my home, miles from where he lived.

11

The energy levels in the kitchen exploded as Nana and I rushed to tidy up in a wild panic, almost bumping into each other in the process.

"He's coming here?" I said out loud, mainly to stop myself from repeating it in my head.

"That's what the email said." Nana was at the sink, rinsing the teapot. Loretta wiped the table as I put the leftovers back in the fridge. "You had better go and shower," Nana said over her shoulder. "And try to do something with your hair."

I knew things were serious because Nana never mentioned my hair. It was off-limits. I looked over at Loretta, who shrugged and traipsed out of the kitchen. My personal life was outside of her professional obligations at the B&B.

"I have beds to make," she said.

I took a last look at the clock and ran upstairs.

Under the hot water, I scrubbed myself clean and rinsed my hair, wondering how I was going to deal with Campbell, here, in person. The coffee shop meeting had been awkward and I wasn't keen to repeat the experience. I was in my comfort zone, away from city life. His email had seemed chatty.

Hi Isla, I'm in your area on Friday and thought I'd pop by for a coffee. It'll be just after breakfast, around 11 am. See you, Campbell

As I dried myself, I studied myself in the mirror. Of all the faults I could find in myself, I liked my body. It was long and lean, and I wondered if Campbell would like it too. I imagined myself and Campbell lying in this room, on this bed, kissing and...

I laughed out loud at the wildness of the idea, and my laughter echoed back at me like the world was laughing in my face.

I pulled on my jeans. Girls like me didn't date men like Campbell. It was that simple. Campbell dated women like Sophie, hard-nosed, highly groomed and with what used to be called 'good breeding'. My heritage could be traced back to a long line of factory workers and fishermen. A heritage I was proud of, but it wasn't a fit for someone like Campbell who probably had lords and ladies in his ancestry line.

I imagined his dad sending him on a mercy mission because the Head of Marketing, Sophie, couldn't function without my support, and continued coffee runs.

"Go and get her, Campbell, Sophie needs caffeine and her dry-cleaning collected."

I was so nervous, I tried to calm my nerves in the traditional Barker way, with tea. I sat at the kitchen table, nursing a cup of chamomile tea.

Nana had cleared the kitchen table, leaving flour, sugar and butter out. This was a pointed reminder that I had fresh scones to make for the afternoon tea. I did some maths in my head and reasoned that I'd have to usher Campbell away by 1:30 pm at the latest so I could walk Charlie and be back to bake scones in time. Rich people might not have a clock to adhere to, but Barker women did.

The doorbell made my stomach drop to my feet, and it took all of my strength to stand up. Pulling myself to my full height, I felt my knees shaking, in danger of *literally* letting me down. I tried to reframe Campbell's visit as completely normal, picturing a scene where he popped in all the time, casually dropping by for a coffee, a hobnob. I dragged myself to the front door and swung it open.

I caught my breath. There he was. Looking as perfect as ever, but so much more handsome than I remembered him. His shirt was a checked blue, tucked into jeans, and his designer sunglasses were pushed up over his thick dark hair. He smiled and my heart melted like butter, dripping from my chest and pooling around my toes.

"Hey, Isla!" His tone was breezy like we were best friends and did this all the time.

I stared at him, then realised I was staring and jumped back.

"Campbell, hi! Come in!" I sounded robotic but it was the best I could do, stunned into mechanical mode while I digested the fact that he was here. Larger than life, breathing, walking along the Sea Colme Cottage hallway, looking at dad's beach photography saying, "This is nice, great photos, who took these?"

"My dad," I said, pausing from my march towards the kitchen to look at the photos. It had been a while since I'd had a good look and I realised that dad had changed a few. I cringed when I saw one of me, smiling on the beach in a striped swimsuit, walking to the water, dragging a kayak behind me. My hamster cheeks were full, and my hair straggled with salt water, but thankfully it covered half of my face.

Campbell's eyes followed mine and he moved to stand beside me.

"This one is lovely," he said.

I turned my head a tiny amount to study him. His eyes darted over the photograph and he wore a grin.

"I didn't know you kayaked."

I nodded. How would he?!

"Living so close to the beach, it's normal," I stammered. "Do you?"

I knew what his answer would be, of course. Campbell was probably skilled in every water sport.

"I haven't tried it."

I turned to him in surprise. He shook his head.

"I have a bit of a fear of open water." He looked sheepish.

Growing up by the sea, I'd never met anyone scared of water. It was so much a part of our lives. I felt like a layer of Campbell Maclean had just slipped away. I didn't know this version of him. It gave me inner confidence.

"Maybe I could teach you…" The words were out of my mouth before I had a chance to think about what they might entail. Me and Campbell going out to sea. K-A-Y-A-K-I-N-G…

I mean, it wasn't a bad thing.

"I'd like that," he said softly.

Campbell turned his head to face me and I tilted my head up so that I could fully enjoy *The Look*. I had never been this close to him before, and standing in the Sea Colme Cottage hallway together felt strange. My stomach filled with butterflies and I swallowed, not sure what was happening.

Standing with Campbell's eyes locked with mine felt like a fairytale. Just a couple of hours ago my face had been inches-close to another, very different, but equally attractive man. I took a moment to wonder whose life I was living. Was I in the middle of one of those lengthy and complicated dreams? Was I about to wake up with the sudden chill of morning reality?

"There you are!"

Nana's chirpy voice startled the two of us, making us jump apart like we were guilty of something.

Colour spread from my neck to my cheeks and I faced Nana with a beetroot-red face. She raised an eyebrow and looked past me to Campbell, who seemed equally red-faced. Charlie came rushing through, barking loudly and jumping up at me. He always acted like he hadn't seen me in weeks.

"This must be the famous Charlie!" Campbell stepped forward and offered the back of his hand for Charlie to smell before getting a nudge of approval for further affection. I watched the two of them together and my heart somersaulted.

"I have just put the kettle on, would you like a cuppa? Campbell, isn't it?" Nana oozed charm, and I dared Campbell to refuse.

"You must be Isla's gran!" Campbell stepped forward, his hand outstretched towards Nana. Charlie entwined himself with Campbell's legs.

"This is Nana," I said, trying to offer the too-late introduction. The hallway fell silent as Nana looked him up and down before eventually smiling.

"You can call me Mabel," she said, waving his hands away, and patting him on the arm instead. "No formalities here, lad." She looked at Campbell and then back at me. "Why don't you show our guest into the kitchen?"

She winked at me, and I grinned at her ironic formality. Everyone called Nana, Nana. I didn't know anyone in this town who called her Mabel.

"Isla?" Nana prompted.

I lurched forward, brushing my hair out of my eyes.

"Do come into the kitchen, Campbell," I said, holding my arm out to show the way.

Campbell followed with Charlie at his heels.

I tried to ignore the heat in my face that hadn't subsided.

12

"When she was five," Nana said, talking about me as if I wasn't sitting right next to her, cringing, "she announced to us all that she wanted to be a writer, and I was delighted."

I tried to slide further into my seat at the kitchen table. I didn't want to spoil Nana's fun — stories like these meant she liked Campbell — so I smiled, nodded and hid my face when things got too awful.

"I only found out recently she was a writer," Campbell said and shot a look at me. "Very talented, a way with words. The whole office thought so." Campbell was smiling.

I cringed even more.

"She is good," Nana said, "she's won prizes, competitions. Though she'd never tell you."

I felt my face flush red with embarrassment. I rarely told anyone about my writing successes, it seemed like I was showing off. But at University I'd been encouraged to enter competitions and was surprised when I won a few. Nana loved to tell anyone who would listen.

I didn't know Campbell well enough to gauge what he thought, so I found myself stealing looks at his face to determine what he was thinking. I also searched for clues as to why he was here. Although it felt like he'd turned up out of the blue, he had emailed three days ago to let me know he was coming. I just didn't know *why* he had to come in person. He could have emailed me the job details.

He nursed a cup of coffee and listened to Nana, his laughter only encouraging her further.

I loved hearing myself described from Nana's perspective. Her tales were laced with affection, and I felt safe, ensconced in her love.

"Right, Isla," Nana announced at the end of her impromptu *Jackanory* session, pressing her hands into the table to stand up. "Why don't you give Campbell the grand tour of the place, the beach, and then you'll have to start the scones."

She winked at me. I was glad to have her emotional support. Nana could see Campbell's visit had unsettled me. I usually felt so at home at Sea Colme Cottage, it was my haven. But now my biggest crush was at the very core of it, sitting at our kitchen table, laughing with my Nana.

Charlie had sat up in his bed at the sound of the word beach, and when he saw me stand he came forward wagging his tail.

"I guess Charlie likes the beach?" Campbell said, ruffling his fur.

"He does, he's a city boy during the week, and a beach boy at the weekend."

I cringed. Why had I said that?

I busied myself getting Charlie's lead and picking up my coat.

"Nice to meet you, Mabel," Campbell said to Nana.

Nana smiled. "You don't get away that easily," she said. "I'll see you after your walk on the beach for a quick lesson in making scones. I used to run a scone school, you know." Nana folded a tea towel and looked proud.

Caught out by her sudden expectation that he would stay, Campbell looked at me for support.

"Nana, maybe Campbell has things to get on with," I said. A man like that did not want to come back to the kitchen and make scones!

"Nonsense," Nana said. "You want to learn how to make the best scone, don't you lad?"

I turned to Campbell, ready to reassure him that he didn't have to, but I saw him beaming. "I would love to!"

"Grand," said Nana, shooing us out of the kitchen. "See you both in an hour!"

Charlie strained on his lead as we crossed the road to the beach. There was a slight breeze in the air, and I cursed myself for not grabbing my fleece. I couldn't go back now, Nana had made it clear we were to walk for an hour.

"It's a quaint place," Campbell said, breaking the silence.

I looked back towards Sea Colme Cottage and nodded. The affection I had for our home was huge. Those four walls held our family, memories old and new.

"It is. We're very lucky." I looked over at Campbell. "What about you? Do you have a place like Sea Colme Cottage?"

His face tensed briefly.

"No, we have something very modern and big." He rolled his eyes. "It's very dull."

I wondered if he wanted me to feel sorry for him, the millionaire's son. I knew enough about the world to know that just because you had money, it didn't mean you were happy. Sea Colme had lots of wealthy guests from all over the world, and they all told tales of their lives. They loved Sea Colme for its character and simple charm and, of course, the Barker hospitality.

"Well," I said, unleashing an excited Charlie and watching him gallop away. "This is my favourite part of North Berwick."

I spread my arms out wide, proud of our town. The beach was my happy place, and standing on this beach with Campbell, my nerves in my chest, did nothing to quell my elation.

"It's quite a beach!" Campbell said, looking at the miles of sandy beach ahead of us.

"Sometimes you can walk for hours, and not see a soul. Although this is the most crowded part. The golf course is that way, and the seabirds that way." I pointed left and right. "And that," I gestured out to the sea, "is the famous Bass Rock."

Campbell nodded his appreciation of the landscape. I hugged my arms around myself. I should have brought my jacket.

``You're cold," Campbell said, slipping his coat from his shoulders without missing a beat.

"Oh no," I said, shivering. "I'm used to it."

"I insist. Can't have you catching a chill." Campbell came forward and put his jacket over my shoulder. I moved my arms to fit snugly inside and he stepped closer to zip me up.

We were close again. I avoided his eyes this time.

"There," he said, putting his hands on both of my shoulders, leaving me with no choice but to look up and meet his eyes.

There it was again. *The Look,* those green pools of his searching mine.

I looked right back, searching for my answers.

"Why are you here, Campbell?"

It was out before I could stop myself. "You could have emailed the job spec."

He didn't miss a beat.

"I wanted to see you," he said, his gaze soft.

My eyes widened in shock. I pictured us from above, standing on the beach, looking for all intents and purposes like lovers sharing a secret. Not strangers who knew almost nothing about each other.

The breeze was picking up and his black hair flapped. I reached up and smoothed it down. As I brought my hand back down, he turned his head and his lips grazed the inside of my wrist.

My eyes met his and he held my gaze.

He was going to kiss me.

Campbell Maclean was on my beach and he was going to kiss me! I stared into his eyes, daring him to.

A bark jolted us back to reality. Charlie was standing in front of us. He must have run the length of the beach and back again.

We sprung apart.

"Charlie!" I cajoled, reaching down to rub his back. "Let's go!"

I took a huge step forward, hoping Campbell would follow. Part of me thought he would come to his senses and say he had to leave. When I felt his body step in close beside me, I relaxed. I had no idea what was happening, but the butterflies had thankfully subsided.

We walked Charlie to the golf courses at the western end of the town, chatting constantly, me pointing out places of interest and Campbell asking questions. It was like I'd known him all my life as if he'd always been there, walking with Charlie and me on the beach and yet he felt like a stranger from another planet at the same time.

Two figures ahead stopped me in my tracks.

Tim and Chloe were walking along the beach towards us. I did a quick scan for Charlie. Had he sniffed out Tim?

He was playing at the water's edge. If I called him now, we could double back along the high street and miss them both completely. I had to be quick — if Charlie caught a whiff of Tim, I'd have to stop and chat.

I whistled and watched as Charlie came running.

"Let's walk along the high street, you should see it." I directed Campbell, sneaking a look back to see where Tim and Chloe were. Thankfully they hadn't seen us and I manoeuvred Campbell and Charlie along the path.

"Who was that?"

"Who?" I said, my face flushed.

"Whoever you were avoiding back there," he smiled. "You seemed to tense up and wanted to run away."

How had he noticed that?

"Oh…" I thought about making up a story quickly of them being old-school friends but settled on telling the truth. "It's my ex and his new girlfriend." I hung my head.

"Don't you get on?" Campbell pressed.

"It's fine. It's just — " I stopped, not knowing what to say. I was over Tim, a little bruised from his rejection, but I had no feelings for him anymore.

Campbell spoke again, his voice soft. "Did he upset you?"

I shook my head. I liked that Campbell cared but he didn't need to on my part.

"It's Charlie," I blurted out. I could feel tears threatening.

"What about Charlie?" Campbell's voice was still soft. I liked it.

I attempted to explain.

"When we broke up, I tried so hard to maintain contact between Charlie and Tim. But Tim didn't want to keep in touch. He said it would confuse Charlie." I could hear my voice catching.

"That makes sense," Campbell said, instinctively reaching to pat Charlie as we walked.

"But now he wants to look after him. He asked me if he could take him for a few hours." I blinked back a tear. I was fiercely protective of Charlie.

Campbell said nothing and I carried on talking.

"I don't want Charlie to go to him," I watched Charlie walking along, wagging his tail, tongue lolling out of his mouth.

"Why?"

"Because Charlie's not Tim's dog anymore. He gave up that right." I could hear the anger in my words and stopped myself from saying anything else. I didn't want Campbell to think I was unreasonable.

"Maybe he felt guilty about breaking up and left something behind for you." Campbell shrugged. I started to say that wasn't possible and stopped. Tim wasn't a bad person. He'd been a good boyfriend, we'd wanted different things and although it was hurtful, breaking up had been the right thing to do.

We turned the corner and found ourselves at the top of the High Street. It looked especially pretty today and the sight of it lifted my spirits. Shop awnings flapped in the wind and people moved in and out of the road to avoid the slow trickle of cars. Some of the shops had started to put up their festive decorations.

"Well, this is it, the famous North Berwick High Street!"

"Very nice," said Campbell, appraising its qualities.

We walked along, looking into shop windows, and gave Campbell a rundown of the shops and their owners. I wanted him to like North Berwick. We stopped at the second cafe to read the menus.

"I should have asked if you were hungry?"

"No, sorry." Campbell looked distracted, which made me a little nervous. "I'm not, I love cooking and I find it interesting reading menus, seeing what other chefs add to theirs." He turned to me, his face a little drained of colour. "Is that weird?" He raised an eyebrow and gave a small smirk.

I reached out and patted him on the arm, feeling the spark that shot through my hands.

"It's lovely that you cook," I said encouragingly. "I feel like I grew up in the kitchen. Watching my parents, or Nana, make some concoction or another." I cast my mind back to that happy place, almost smelling the delicious aromas of the Sea Colme kitchen. Pies, pastries, soups, stews, and an exotic array of cakes and spices…

"The kitchen is my happy place. Over lockdown, I discovered a love of cooking. I'm always looking for new recipes," Campbell said. "One day I'd like to have my own restaurant. I should cook for you sometime."

"I'd like that," I said, watching Campbell's face as he turned to me briefly. We shared a small smile.

"Isla, I wonder…"

"Isla!" The echo of my name caused me to turn. My stomach sank. Crossing the road ahead of us, was Tim and Chloe.

I groaned. It was far too late to try and hide.

13

To say meeting Tim and Chloe with Campbell was awkward would be an understatement. The four of us stood on the street corner, talking over each other and trying to fill in the gaps of silence.

Chloe was just as smiley as she'd been when I met her at the station a week ago. I sensed there wasn't a bad bone in her body, and she'd earned brownie points again by reaching down and fussing over Charlie. And Charlie, good boy that he was, was lapping up the attention, as I fully expected him to.

Tim gave Campbell a visual appraisal and turned to me.

"Did you decide when would be good for us to have Charlie?"

I furrowed my brows.

"Sorry, Tim, I never said — "

"Look at him," Tim interrupted. "He's happy, he'll be fine."

He turned to look at Chloe and I followed his gaze. Charlie was nuzzling into her neck, something I thought he only did with me. I pulled protectively on his lead and he looked up at me, his tongue still lolling happily out of his mouth. I loosened my grip guiltily.

Maybe it was time to let Charlie back to Tim occasionally. Maybe it would be good for him.

"I'm sorry to interrupt," I heard Campbell saying. "But we have an appointment we need to get to."

I spun my head to look at Campbell, grateful for his intervention. I needed to get away from Tim while I gathered my thoughts.

"Nice to see you both again," I said, as Campbell steered me away and along the street.

"I'll message you," Tim called out, but I didn't look back. Instead, I let Campbell lead me along the street.

"Are you okay?" he asked, as soon as we were a few steps away.

I took a deep breath. Was I okay? I was over Tim, that was clear, and seeing him again with Chloe seemed normal. But still, his claim on Charlie unnerved me.

"Isla?" Campbell prompted me.

I shook my head and reached forward to pat Charlie.

"I know he's a dog, and most people will think I'm crazy, but he's my family."

"People make mistakes, all the time," Campbell said. "Perhaps he's in a better place now. I'm sure you are too?"

I felt torn — how could he be defending Tim?! But the fact that Campbell was defending someone he didn't even know made me think he was a good guy. I liked that, even if I didn't agree with him.

"You must think I'm an awful person," I said, turning to glance at him. "I usually say yes all the time."

He shook his head.

"Of course I don't think that."

I understood what he meant, that people could change. Had I got it wrong, had Tim left Charlie with me to ease my heartbreak? If so, it must have been hard on him to do that.

"Maybe he's trying to impress his new girlfriend?" Campbell added. "Men do silly things to impress women." He wiggled his eyebrows and I couldn't help but smile. "Talking of which, I think we're going to be late for Scone School if we don't pick up the pace."

His words made me giggle and his suggestion that he was trying to impress me left me feeling warm inside. I pictured Nana back in the kitchen at Sea Colme, with bowls, flour and butter at the ready.

"Let's cut back down to the beach, it's a more direct route," I said, pointing to the next turn.

"I'd like to come back here though," Campbell said looking along the length of the street. He turned to me and smiled, "Perhaps we could get lunch at some time?" I nodded, somehow not registering that this sounded like he was asking me out on a date… "The Italian place looks good — or Barnacles? It seems a little run down, but quite charming."

I felt instinctively protective over Barnacles.

"The owners are older," I said. "They've been running it for years. We are not looking forward to the day when they sell up and leave."

Campbell craned his neck to look back at Barnacles, with its shabby-chic frontage that locals knew was just shabby.

"Looks like a nice place, great location," He said kindly, pursing his lips. He looked back to Luciano's menu.

Of course, he wouldn't be interested in somewhere run-down and rough at the edges like Barnacles when there was delicious Italian food on offer in a shiny, modern restaurant virtually right next door. My stomach was starting to rumble thinking about Luciano's spicy spaghetti vongole.

"This is our favourite place to eat," I admitted. "Mum and Dad know the owners. Well, everyone knows everyone here. It's that sort of place."

Campbell took a long look up and down the High Street.

"It's perfect," he said with a smile. "I adore Italian food, it's my favourite thing to cook. Maybe next time?"

His voice softened and I nodded shyly, although my heart leapt at the thought of a next time.

An hour later we were back at Sea Colme Cottage, waiting for a batch of scones to come out of the oven. The kitchen was full of sugary baking smells and Charlie was thumping his tail against the floor as he waited for scraps of whatever we were cooking.

"You're a natural, lad," Nana had said to Campbell as he'd worked the scone mixture earlier. "Your fingers were made for baking."

I'd looked across at Campbell. Campbell Maclean, who I'd seen in high-powered meetings with high-profile clients, his face unreadable in the wake of Nana's praise.

"Coming from you, that's a huge compliment." Campbell had smiled. "I do enjoy cooking. I was telling Isla that I'd love to have my own restaurant one day."

"Well, I can vouch for your talent," Nana had said, "You should follow your heart, lad — doing something you love doesn't feel like work at all. That big city life, it's not all it's cracked up to be." She shook her head and touched Campbell's shoulder.

I watched the two of them now, shoulder-to-shoulder at the sink as they tidied away the utensils and bowls. Campbell was chatting away to Nana like he'd known her his whole life. I'm not sure anyone in Campbell's world had ever encouraged him to follow his heart.

"Now," Nana said, drying her hands on a tea towel and leaving Campbell to finish up. "Let's get a fresh pot ready to have with some sandwiches, and try this next batch of scones."

As Nana picked up the teapot it slipped from her hands. Immediately Campbell leaned forward to catch it.

"I can do that," he said, his hands around the teapot. "If I may?"

"Are you okay Nana?" I tried to keep my voice light — if Nana caught a whiff of concern she'd be cross.

"Of course," she said, letting Campbell take the teapot. "It needs a rinse, cold water first, then a dash of boiled water from the kettle. Good tea needs a warm pot."

As Campbell walked over to the sink with the teapot and his instructions, Nana winked at me and gave me a thumbs-up.

I covered the giggle that was about to escape my mouth. She'd done it on purpose, and I had no cause for concern. It looked like he'd won Nana's approval.

We ate a sandwich each and then a scone each, fresh from the oven, slathered with butter and Nana's homemade apricot jam.

Campbell thanked us both for our company, and my heart thudded. I knew he'd have to leave eventually, but I hadn't made myself ready for him to go just yet. Nana said she'd pack some scones for him, and although I didn't want him to go, I was feeling exhausted from being on edge all morning. Hanging around with your crush is more tiring than you might expect — the exertion of listening, asking, chatting, guessing and judging and assessing. Everything else in my life had been on hold, I hadn't answered emails, given Charlie much attention, or done my share of the tidying up. I'd have to spend the afternoon catching up before I sat down to write, and I didn't like being behind. I decided to do my daily quota of writing first, the emails could wait.

Campbell gave Nana a quick peck on the cheek as he left, and me a slightly longer one as we said goodbye at the door. I stood waving for as long as I could, then closed the heavy door with a sigh, touching my cheek again.

"Well?" Nana prompted as soon as I was back in the kitchen. "Was it everything you expected?"

I couldn't even form words to articulate how I felt. How *did* I feel?

Nana left me to drift back down to earth. "You gather your thoughts," she said. "I'm off for a read." She hung the tea towel on the oven door handle and left the kitchen.

'Off for a read' was Nana's code for 'going to nap'. She'd take a book to her favourite seat in the conservatory, and hours later we'd find her dozing contentedly.

I went up to my desk, Charlie following at my heels. He settled himself on my bed, while I got straight into my stretch of daily writing.

Time passed so quickly when I was writing.

By four o'clock the guests still hadn't arrived, so I decided to take Charlie out for an afternoon walk. This time we had the beach all to ourselves. We walked the length of the sand, not seeing a soul. The tide was out and Charlie ran for the stick I threw and brought it back to me, a constant loop of energy and exertion.

I truly felt relaxed and happy right at that moment, with wet sand on my shoes, salt water making my curly hair even curlier and wild, and Charlie's sandy wet paw prints on my jeans from his jumping at my side.

I could easily get used to a life like this and remembered my mission to get Mairi to move back here.

But what about Campbell? I still didn't know what was happening there. And look at the effect he'd had on me! Just his presence here had left me uptight and nervous. As handsome, powerful and sexy as Campbell was, he made me jumpy. Every look, every touch, had made me jump out of my skin. In a book, the author would want me to believe this was sexy and electric, and I should be over the moon, but the reality was — it felt *strange. I* felt strange. Not myself. Surely that wasn't right?

The late afternoon sunshine broke through the clouds, and the wind whipped my hair up with sand from the beach. As we turned back towards Sea Colme, Charlie trotting obediently beside me, I felt more like myself.

I pushed through the huge front door and breathed in the familiar scent of home.

The atmosphere in the hallway was the first signal that something was amiss. The second was Nana standing next to the computer looking dishevelled like she'd been woken from her afternoon nap. Nobody ever woke Nana from a nap! An angry-looking woman stood next to her, leaning over and jabbing at the computer screen, and a man was tapping and scrolling on the screen of his mobile phone.

"Isla!" Nana exclaimed, looking simultaneously relieved and distraught. "Thank God you're back. I'm having a disaster."

All three of them watched me with impatient eyes as I struggled out of my coat.

14

"It won't click to the next screen," Nana whispered, her voice thick with confusion and frustration. She was clicking the mouse repeatedly and without success.

I took off my coat and smiled at the couple, my inherent hospitality mode coming to the fore. From a young age I had been working at Sea Colme, and it came naturally to me to switch to host mode.

"Hello there, thanks for being patient — it looks like we're having difficulty with the computer." I slid behind the counter and took over the mouse, with Nana breathing over my shoulder. "Let me see if I can sort it." The booking system would only allow me to click on one screen, and when I pressed enter, nothing happened.

The man looked hot under the collar and the woman's face still wore a scowl of anger. I willed the screen to spring to life and used a combination of keys to reset the program. It felt like an hour passed before the booking platform reloaded.

I smiled at the woman. "Okay! Can I take your name please?"

"The booking is under Smith," the man said, the woman held her head high in the air.

I clicked through the check-in process.

"We usually offer an afternoon tea with freshly baked scones ready to welcome you." I smiled, hoping to ease their day. "But perhaps because of the lateness you'd rather go straight to dinner? I could make a booking somewhere locally for you?"

The couple looked at each other. The woman shook her head.

"We're not late!" She scowled.

I apologised as gently as I could. "I didn't mean to infer that you were late, just the late hour — "

She shook her head and snapped at her husband.

"I need a lie down first. Gerald, can you take over?"

I smiled as benevolently as I could, as I realised that the computer had frozen again, just as it had for Nana.

"That's what it was doing for me," she muttered.

I furrowed my brows. The check-in wasn't just stuck, it also wasn't registering the name.

"Is the reservation definitely under Smith?" I asked carefully. The woman's eyes looked like I had just cursed her firstborn child. "Perhaps you could spell Smith for me?"

The couple looked at me open-mouthed, then at each other. I caught the rise of the woman's eyebrow although it was not intended for me to see.

"What a terrible welcome," the woman said sharply. "I've never been treated like this."

Over the years we'd had plenty of mishaps, but rude customers were rare. Mum and dad prided themselves on the level of service they gave at Sea Colme and our reviews reflected it. I couldn't bear the idea that they might come back and find a bad review while I was looking after the place. I plastered a smile on my face.

"I'm so sorry, the technology is at fault here. We recently switched to a new booking system. Nana, why don't you settle Mr and Mrs Smith with afternoon tea while I sort this out?"

Nana nodded and gestured towards the dining room.

"I don't want afternoon tea, I want to lie down. I have a headache," the woman barked, turning away from the counter. Nana and I looked at each other and then back towards the couple.

"Please," the man said, coming forward, his voice lowered. "Perhaps we could get the room key while you sort out your booking system?"

"Absolutely," I nodded, handing the key over. "I'll sort this out and you can go to relax."

The man took the key gratefully.

"I'll go and settle her in." The man scooped an arm around his wife. "Norma, this way."

Nana and I watched as the man led her away. I closed the computer down and fired it up again.

"Maybe a restart will help." I shrugged. Mum and dad's laptop was old and I had been on at them to get a newer one, but it hadn't ever seemed to be a priority for them. As Nana and I fussed over the computer we saw the man approaching the counter again.

Hopeful he didn't have a complaint about the room, I smiled as if we'd never met. A fresh start.

"Hello, thanks for earlier." He nodded.

"No problem, it was all our fault." I nodded, grateful not to be defusing another emotional bomb. The man loitered.

"Was there something else?" I smiled.

"Perhaps I could have a separate room?" The ends of his moustache folded into the creases in his cheeks when he smiled. It was very endearing.

I hesitated, confused.

"I'm so sorry, I didn't realise you'd booked two rooms!" I felt my cheeks flush.

"Oh, we had emailed!" His smile seemed embarrassed. "We're not together, you see. We're old friends, here for a reunion."

Out of the corner of my eye, I could see Nana doubting this scenario. My hands hovered over the keys rack. Without the computer, there was no way to easily check which rooms were empty. I went over the number of breakfast tables I'd served earlier in my mind and decided which one should be empty.

I reached for a key — a front room with beautiful views of the sea, one of my favourites. Guests never failed to enthuse about its outlook.

"Will you be paying for both rooms?" I asked.

"No, I believe Norma prepaid for hers, so it's just mine to settle."

Nana busied herself with papers behind me as I took a payment from the man's card, and handed him his receipt with as much professionalism as I could muster. After the awkwardness earlier I wanted to ensure smoother service from here on out.

"Would you like afternoon tea while your friend rests? The dining room is rather cosy and the views are lovely as the sun sets."

The man smiled.

"Oh, charming. That sounds perfect. Thank you, dear." He tipped his cap to me, as Nana led him away, apologising again for the difficulties earlier.

When they had gone I stared at the desk. The booking system was still refusing to work and I needed it — I had Christmas market emails to reply to, and applications from suppliers to check on. Mum had reassured me that everything was in hand, but I wanted to do a good job for her.

I needed her blue notebook, which held all her passwords. If I could find that, then I could log into the system from my laptop while I got the older computer fixed.

I opened all of the drawers and looked through them, each full of instruction manuals that I imagined dad had put there for safekeeping and tourist attraction leaflets. The bottom drawer wouldn't close and kept jamming on something. I pushed harder hoping to loosen whatever was lodged there, then fished my hand to the back and pulled out the offending article.

I gasped.

In my hand was a photo of all of us, taken outside Sea Colme during the lockdown. Mum, dad, Nana, me, and Tim, who was holding the cutest puppy — Charlie.

While all of us Barkers were beaming into the camera, Tim was looking in another direction. I peered closer at his face and realised he was gazing lovingly at Charlie, who was gazing up at him. It took me aback. This was the relationship between man and dog I had remembered.

In my mind I had thought Tim hadn't cared for Charlie at all if he could have given him up, yet here was his love on full display. It was clear that Tim had adored Charlie, no matter how much he must have tried to hide it at the time.

I felt a pang of sadness picturing Tim's face when we broke up. It must have been hard on him, knowing he was breaking my heart. To be kind, and to make things easier for me in the separation, he had given up Charlie.

I knew what I had to do. Before I second-guessed myself, I took out my phone and sent a text message.

Nana shuffled along the hallway, pulling her coat around her shoulders. She saw me standing amid the mess and disarray of the office counter.

"What on earth are you doing?"

The desk was covered in the contents of the drawers from my hunt for mum's little blue book.

"What are you searching for?" Nana peered over the mess.

"Mum's blue notebook." I sighed. "If I find that, I'll find her passwords and, voila! I can log into the email account from my laptop. Problem solved."

Nana smiled. "Just one problem," she said.

I groaned. What had I overlooked?

"Your Mum takes that notebook everywhere."

I smacked my forehead. Of course, she'd have taken it on her trip with her!

"It's not here, is it…" I couldn't disguise my dismay.

Nana shook her head.

"It's not. So you won't find it, no matter how thorough you are. You're going to need a plan B."

15

The following week I sat in Barnacles, staring into my cappuccino, willing a solution to present itself. The booking system was causing havoc and I hadn't heard a peep from Campbell despite him having my number, but that wasn't my main focus.

Tim and Chloe had picked up Charlie that morning and I had planned to keep myself busy instead of moping around the house. I knew I'd only be listening out for the door every time it opened or closed if I stayed behind, so I had to escape.

I didn't want to go to the beach, in case I bumped into the three of them, so I'd settled myself here with a consoling coffee and a slice of Hetty's famous date and walnut slice.

I longed for Mairi to be here, so I could talk through my realisation that Tim and Charlie should be together. I looked at my phone but knew it was no use trying to call her, it was midweek, and she'd be far too busy for a phone call. She wasn't due back in town for another week, so I had no chance of catching up at the weekend either.

I was conscious of taking up precious space at the cafe and leaning on Burt and Hetty's good nature. Small businesses like ours relied on custom, and it was up to us to provide it. I was about to order lunch to justify staying when a voice interrupted my thoughts.

"Is this seat free?"

I turned to see Johnny, the guy I'd met at the beach, hovering next to me.

"Oh hi — "

He pointed to the bench. "Can I join you?"

I moved along the bench, making room on the table for him. Johnny settled himself into a seat and looked around the cafe.

"I like this place," he said, looking around the cafe and giving his approval like I'd suggested meeting there.

I nodded, unsure if I was going to be good company.

"It's a North Berwick institution." I smiled but wished I had said I was busy. With the problems at the B&B and Charlie being away, I wasn't in the mood for aimless conversation.

He signalled for Hetty's attention and she shuffled over, bringing another coffee I hadn't asked for.

"On the house," she winked.

I listened as they chatted, Burt had a meeting with another buyer, but they weren't too hopeful, then after Hetty drifted away we sat in silence for a moment.

As I sipped my coffee I sensed Johnny watching me.

"You don't have to tell me," he said, "but I sense that something's up."

I nodded.

"Yeah, you could say that." I filled my cheeks and exhaled the air. "I'm having a bad day."

He leaned his head to the side and looked at me. He was watching me, but I didn't feel judged. It felt comforting.

"Do you want to talk about it?"

I thought about it, then nodded.

"It sounds daft," I admitted.

"Try me." He smiled.

I wondered how to explain my hurt at leaving my dog with someone who made me unhappy. Then I realised he didn't have his dog with him.

"Where's Pickles?"

He raised his eyebrows.

"That's the reason I'm here, hiding," he said. "She's back at the flat. With my ex."

"You're kidding?" I couldn't stop myself from bursting out.

He nodded grimly.

"Every Tuesday lunch hour. She works nearby then and can pop in. It's not ideal, but I couldn't deny Pickles the time. She loves it."

I stared at Johnny in disbelief.

'What?!"

I shook my head. "I can't believe it. That's why I'm here too!"

Johnny raised an eyebrow.

"Because Pickles is having a playdate?" he teased.

I leaned across the table to playfully swat his arm.

"Charlie is with Tim, my ex!" I said.

"Well, isn't that a coincidence!"

Johnny looked at me for a few seconds too long. I stared back at him, feeling again that same connection we'd had at the beach. Then, looking into each other's eyes, we started laughing. A slow giggle at first, which grew to a deeper laugh.

"Look at the pair of us," Johnny said, shaking his head. "Lost without our dogs, eating our feelings."

"I can't believe it." I wiped tears of laughter from my eyes. I felt lighter in myself. "I miss him, but to be honest, it wasn't only the situation with Charlie that put me in a grump."

Johnny raised an eyebrow, encouraging me to continue.

I told him about the problems at the B&B, our technical failings and the difficult customers I'd had to deal with while Johnny listened and nodded attentively.

Hetty brought him his food and winked at me again as she walked away.

Johnny took a bite and wiped his mouth with a napkin. "Migraines are awful things," he said, of the woman who'd been so awful the day before. "Seems like she didn't know how to cope."

"That's a good way of looking at it," I said. "What makes you so wise?"

Johnny shrugged.

"Oh gosh, not me. I'm not wise. But my aunt is quite a sensitive soul, she gets migraines all the time. I guess I'm used to it."

I looked at him, picking crumbs from his plate, sitting relaxed in Barnacles. In a few short sentences, he'd changed my mood completely.

"Should we get a coffee to go?" I knew I was being forward, but I felt comfortable doing so.

Johnny looked at me and I waited for him to answer. Those gorgeous eyes, his hair framing his face, a smile playing on his lips.

"I'd love to," he said.

We went to the counter together to pay, and he insisted on putting my coffee and cake on his bill.

"Do you have a sweet tooth?" I saw him scanning the trays of sweet treats on the counter. The whole cabinet was full of tray bakes, slices and individual cakes.

"Guilty!" he said good-naturedly. "One of my weaknesses."

"You'll have to try Nana's scones and homemade jam."

"I'd like that," Johnnie smiled. I imagined him in the kitchen, sitting and chatting with Nana. The thought made me smile.

We took our coffees and walked over the south beach, back towards Sea Colme.

"Hello" a voice called, and we both turned our heads to see a woman with pink hair smiling at us.

"Hello, you!" Johnny said, leaving me to pull the woman into a bear hug.

I stood watching them with a stab of jealousy, which I instantly felt silly for, of course, I wouldn't be the only woman in this town who had an eye on Johnny.

But as they sprang apart and the woman looked at me with a friendly smile, I knew instinctively that I had nothing to worry about.

"Have you met Sally?" Johnny said, his arm still around her shoulders.

I smiled and stuck out my hand.

"I haven't, hi Sally, I'm Isla." We shook hands.

"Nice to meet you Isla, I'm glad to see someone finally coaxed Johnny out for a walk."

"Sally and Caleb own Java Lava," Johnny said, ignoring Sally's playful mention of the two of us being together.

"You must pop by for a coffee. I must dash, see you for dinner later Johnny. And Isla, hopefully, I'll see you soon too." Sally said to Johnny and me, making it completely obvious she thought our being together was a date.

"She's nice," I said as Sally rushed away.

"She's brilliant. She and Caleb are working day and night in that cafe to make it a success."

I nodded. "Small businesses are hard work." I knew from holding the reigns at Sea Colme Cottage that things didn't always go smoothly. My mind drifted back to last week's guests. Thankfully the woman had been in a better mood the next day, and her companion had been full of praise as they checked out. I couldn't bear mum and dad getting a bad review.

I looked up and down the beach, wondering what direction to head.

"It's probably best we avoid that end of the beach for a while," Johnny said, articulating what I'd been thinking. I wanted to avoid the north end, and the possibility of bumping into Tim and Chloe walking Charlie.

I was glad when Johnny steered me in the opposite direction.

"This is where we hold the Christmas Market." I stretched my arms out wide, as we reached the spot in front of Sea Colme.

Soon it would be full of stallholders, dad's BBQ, music would be playing and the village would come out in support of all the small businesses.

"What a great spot." Johnny took a sip of his coffee.

"If you like sweet treats, wait until you try Joyce's Sinful Christmas loaf, it's sweet and savoury," I said. My mouth almost watered at the thought of it, heavily slathered with apricot jam and a wedge of cheese. "And my Mum's cinnamon buns." My mind drifted to mum and dad on their Northern Lights cruise and I felt a wave of love.

"What are they like?" Johnny asked.

"My parents, or the buns?" I said jokingly. "They're great. I've been spoiled."

"I meant the cinnamon buns," Johnny said, an embarrassed smile crossing his lips.

I blushed.

"What about you?" I asked.

"I hit the jackpot," he said, a little stiffly.

Something in his voice rang a distant alarm bell. I knew something was amiss.

"What is it?"

He bowed his head. "I don't often tell people, it makes them take a few steps back." He pursed his lips.

"Go on," I said, as softly as I could, waiting for the devastation that I sensed was coming.

He hesitated and looked out towards the sea.

"My mum passed away a few years ago."

I held my breath. What an awful thing to happen. I looked at Johnny and stepped forward.

"I'm so sorry to hear that." I reached up to touch his cheek and he turned his head, his lips grazing my hand.

"It's been tough," he said. "For all of us. Me, my dad, my little sister."

Without thinking, I pulled Johnny towards me and wrapped my arms around him. I came up to just below his chest and we fitted snugly together like our bodies were made to go alongside each other.

For some unknown reason, I wanted to make him feel secure.

"Why is it that every meeting with you ends up with us canoodling on a beach." Johnny teased from beneath my hair.

I pulled away and playfully swatted him.

"I have nothing to say in my defence." I giggled, stepping backwards a few paces. "I'm so sorry you lost your mum."

We locked eyes and held each other's gaze for a few seconds too long.

Johnny stopped suddenly, and as I turned he reached forward to brush my hair behind my ears. I felt my pulse start to race.

I pulled my head away from him and looked towards Sea Colme. I saw a figure at the dining window. Nana!

I waved, and she disappeared from view. I narrowed my eyes. Why was Nana spying on me? Maybe she wasn't spying on me, but Johnny. She said she'd know 'the One' the minute she saw him.

A thought struck me.

"Do you have time to come and say hello to my Nana?"

Johnny looked at his watch and shook his head.

"Sorry, I can't. It's time for me to get back to Pickles, and Katie."

The sound of his ex-girlfriend's name brought me back to reality. Whatever we'd been feeling on the beach had been quickly washed away by the mention of Katie's name.

"But how about I pop over tomorrow?" he said. "I could take a look at the laptop for you. I'm a bit of a computer whizz…" He smiled at the admission."And I could try those infamous scones?"

I play-swatted him again but this time he moved out of the way and caught my hand.

"They're not infamous," I laughed, as he began pulling me closer to him. "They're famous."

"Whatever you say…" His teasing made me giggle.

We were nose to nose on the beach. He looked me deeply in the eyes, then lifted his chin to plant a small kiss on the end of my nose. I instantly thought of Campbell and a wave of guilt flushed through my body.

"Johnny…" I started to say but he pulled away and smiled at me.

"See you tomorrow?"

I nodded, and we drifted in opposite directions along the beach.

As I waved goodbye I wondered if it was normal to have that much of a connection with someone after only a few meetings. I'd known Tim throughout my childhood — we'd been neighbours and had gone to school together — and that connection hadn't been enough to keep us together.

I wasn't the most seasoned person in romantic notions. My experience of romantic connections came from the movies I watched with Nana, which I knew weren't real. But if they weren't real, why did it feel like they were?

16

By lunchtime the next day, Johnny hadn't arrived at Sea Colme Cottage to check the computer or try one of Nana's scones, despite me telling her that he would.

In anticipation of his visit, I had cleaned everywhere, even rearranging furniture and dusting off the photographs in the hallway. With time on my hands, I went on to prep the afternoon scone baking session by measuring out the flour and cutting the butter into cubes.

I was just about to start fluffing the cushions for the hundredth time when Nana sent me out for a brisk walk with Charlie.

"Enough!" she said. "I need you out from under my feet."

I wondered what I'd done to provoke her, as she wasn't often openly impatient or irritable with people. She didn't seem as keen on Johnny visiting as she had with Campbell.

"Stop pacing the floor, Isla," she said. "He's not coming, you have to accept it. And no amount of cushion plumping will change that."

Although I knew Nana was right, I stomped down the hallway, collected Charlie's lead and escaped the B&B to get some fresh air. The beach was still busy despite it being November, with some day trippers eating fish and chips on the benches and other dog walkers meandering along the shore.

Walking Charlie gave me time to gather my thoughts. It wasn't only Johnny breaking his promise to visit that was causing me anxiety — I had two weeks until mum and dad came home. I wanted everything to be perfect for them. The Christmas Market on the first of December had to go swimmingly. But to get it all arranged I needed to access the computer. Then, we needed the guest booking platform up and running to make sure the B&B kept operating without a hitch — we'd been getting by on a pen-and-paper system I'd set up, but it wasn't ideal. I needed Johnny for that, as much as for any romantic ambition.

I walked Charlie up to the west beach and we watched golfers swinging their clubs for a while. By the time we got back to east beach, I was calmed and returned to the B&B in a much more relaxed state of mind.

To occupy myself, I decided to settle down for my afternoon writing session and got so lost in my thoughts that when the doorbell rang, it made me jump. Johnny was finally here. With a slight spring in my step, I bounded down the stairs.

I opened the door with a huge smile ready on my face and found myself eye-to-eye with Campbell Maclean.

"Hello!" he beamed, holding out a bunch of flowers.

"Campbell!" I gasped, taking the bouquet from him. What was he doing here?

"Weren't you expecting me?" he said, stepping forward to give Charlie a stroke. "I did email…"

I groaned inwardly — why was that computer working so hard to derail my love life?! Why couldn't he text like a normal millennial?

"Our emails aren't quite working," I said as out of the corner of my eye I saw Johnny making his way along the beach. My heart skipped several beats. I quickly ushered Campbell inside and led Charlie back to the kitchen by the collar.

"Hello, Mabel!" Campbell leaned in to hug Nana.

I watched Nana's confused face break into a huge smile as she was kissed on each cheek by Campbell.

"Well this is a surprise," she said, shooting a glance at me. "Isla didn't tell me you were visiting today." Nana ran her hands through her hair, although it was as immaculate as ever.

"I did email," he said, turning to me, a bemused smile on his face, "I have a business meeting nearby and thought you might like a lunch date."

He'd used the word *date*! I shook my head slightly, not yet willing to believe my own ears.

"What a lovely idea!" Nana laughed. "She'd love to go, let me get the teapot warmed and we can have a cuppa while she gets ready," Nana spoke for me.

The front doorbell rang, making me stiffen.

Nana moved to stand behind Campbell and made faces at me. I had no idea what she was trying to say, but it didn't look polite.

"Let me get that," I said, moving towards the hallway. "Nana will look after you, won't you Nana?"

Thankfully Campbell had knelt down and was ruffling Charlie's fur again, so I could mouth at Nana over his head.

"It's Johnny!" I mouthed. Nana frowned. "J-o-h-n-n-y," I said again, stretching my mouth to squeeze the most out of each vowel without using sound.

The penny dropped with Nana, who covered her mouth with her hand to stop herself from gasping.

"You just stay here," I said, trying to sound as casual as I could. Campbell looked up from the floor where he was playing with Charlie.

"Of course..." He smiled.

I almost ran down the hallway and pulled open the front door to see Johnny leaning against the doorpost. He looked as handsome as ever, wearing a dark purple woollen jumper that contrasted against his blonde hair. I had never wanted to be a door post so much in my life. Did Meg Ryan think like this, I wondered?

"You could look more pleased to see me," Johnny said with a laugh in his voice.

I realised my face must be a picture, with all of the romantic thoughts twirling around my head.

"Sorry," I said. "There's been a lot of stuff going on."

Johnny grinned. "Well, I'm here now," he said. "To fix the computer?"

"Of course!"

I led him into the dining room, feeling the air come back into my body as my breathing restabilised. I gestured to the large dining table.

"Have a seat, I'll bring the laptop over."

I watched over his shoulder as Johnny took his jacket off, hooking it over the back of the chair.

"The decor in here is interesting," Johnny said. I nodded and looked around the dining room, with its muted greys and pinks.

'Mum's colour scheme," I said, missing her deeply at that moment. I placed the old laptop in front of him with a thud.

"She's got great taste, I can't wait to meet her," Johnny said, opening the laptop. "Wow, this is a bit of an antique!"

"She's not here," I said, rushing my words.

Johnny started to tap the keyboard.

"I know that," he said, furrowing his brows as if I was crazy. "They're on a Northern Lights cruise, you're looking after the place. Right?"

I laughed nervously.

"Let me get you a coffee," I said, backing out of the room, and leaving Johnny tapping at the laptop keyboard.

In the privacy of the hallway, I leaned against the wall and wished I could just disappear. This was an utter catastrophe! I had to think on my feet. I could probably keep both men separate if they stayed in their respective rooms. But I needed help. Would Nana help? Of course, she would.

In her own way.

Oh god…

I'd arrived back in the kitchen to find Nana alone. Campbell had nipped to the bathroom.

"We can swap over," Nana said, as I babbled about a plan to stop the two men from meeting each other. "I'll pop in and say hello to Johnny now, while you chat with Campbell."

I knew Nana wanted to go and see Johnny to get the measure of him, so I let her go — taking a coffee for Johnny — and waited for Campbell to return.

I swallowed.

Of all the days to pick to visit, why today?

I heard him pad down the stairs from the bathroom, his face beaming as he came back into the kitchen.

"So, Campbell, how are you?" I stuttered.

He turned to face me and it was like seeing a rainbow in a stormy sky as he smiled. I could feel the heat rising up my neck and spreading to my cheeks.

"I forgot something last time," he whispered, moving beside me and lifting his hand to stroke my cheek with one soft, beautiful finger.

I froze. "You did?"

He leaned forward and took my face in both hands, leaving me unable to look away. I could only stare stupidly upward at him. Stunned. Like a rabbit caught in the headlights of *The Look.*

His eyes were like kaleidoscopes, and the more I stared the more the colour changed from green to yellow to blue and gold.

He hadn't messaged in a week. Why was he in my Mum and Dad's kitchen, trying to kiss me? Why? Why why why why?

I lifted my arms up to take his hands away.

"She's here in the kitchen. You can ask her yourself. ." I could hear Nana's voice, growing louder.

"I don't need to ask — " That was Johnny's voice, and I turned and saw him standing in the kitchen doorway, just in front of Nana, the laptop in his arms. His face wore a look of confusion whereas Nana's face was a picture of delight.

I had my hands on Campbell's arms, as he gently cupped my face. We looked like a tableau of lovers about to kiss.

I sprung back from Campbell, pushing his hands away and causing him to look from Johnny to me, and then back at Johnny.

Johnny stood frozen like a statue, staring. I looked down at the floor.

"Hi, I'm Campbell Maclean..." His manners kicked in, as he sprung forward with an outstretched hand.

"Johnny Martin." Johnny's voice was even and dull as he shook Campbell's hand.

From underneath my shamefaced gaze, I watched them complete the ritual of strangers meeting.

"You're here to fix the booking system?" Campbell managed to make it sound like a perfectly normal conversation.

"Yes, he is," Nana said, interjecting herself into the conversation.

"I guess I am." Johnny closed the laptop with a snap, causing me to jump. "That's all sorted," he said. "It was pretty straightforward, just needed a quick reboot."

He stepped forward and placed the computer on the table. I looked up to see his eyes searching mine for answers.

Mine said one word and one word only: Sorry.

"But you need to log back into your booking system," Johnny said, looking away, breaking eye contact. "Which should be simple. Just pop your password in…"

I groaned. That was going to be a problem.

"Nice to meet you, Nana." Johnny smiled at Nana, who seemed unnaturally subdued. Campbell got to call her Mabel, but for Johnny, it was Nana, a fact that wasn't lost on me.

Johnny took a last glance at me, and then at Campbell.

"I'll see myself out," he said, and then he was gone.

Nana looked at me and I looked at her. Had she done this on purpose?

"What a nice guy," Campbell said, saving us the trouble of having to initiate conversation. "Now, are we having some tea?"

17

I was woken up the next morning by Charlie licking my face. I must have slept past his breakfast time as this wasn't his normal wake-up call.

I pushed him away as gently as I could and checked my phone. I registered a text message from Mairi and nothing from Johnny, although I'd sent him two last night, thanking him for fixing the computer and trying to explain about Campbell.

I spent a few minutes tickling Charlie under his ears; I didn't want to hurt his feelings either.

My mind lurched back to the day before. Yesterday was a disaster. An out-and-out disaster. I doubted I'd see Johnny again after he caught Campbell and me together. Although it wasn't what it looked like.

At the time.

Definitely not at the time.

Campbell had seemed blissfully unaware of any awkwardness when Johnny had left. Then as we were having a cup of tea, his phone bleeped and he announced that he was sorry, but he had to go to an urgent meeting.

I walked him to the door and when I leaned past him to open it he moved quickly, taking me back in his arms and pressing his lips to kiss me. Mine unashamedly met his.

With our lips together, he manoeuvred me so I was pressed up against the wall — or had I pulled him? I couldn't be sure.

For that brief moment, we were as one in the Sea Colme Cottage hallway. I lost all sense of space and time. That kiss represented every time he'd walked past my desk, every time I'd stood next to him in the elevator, every look, every smile, every smirk, every bit of hunger I had for him, and from the ferocity of his kiss I sensed it was the same for him.

Campbell had finally pulled his lips away from mine, and we leaned back against the opposite walls, our breaths coming hot and fast, his chest heaving, his normally perfect hair messy, and mine... well, I could only guess at what mine looked like. I ruffled my fringe and he reached out his hand, gently, with care, to brush it aside.

"I love your hair," he whispered.

We stared at each other, slightly breathless.

What had he just said?

"I have to go, otherwise..." He leaned in and kissed me again. Hungrily. Then he was gone.

I sat a little dazed in the kitchen with Nana who had shaken her head sadly when I told her what had happened.

"Nana, Campbell kissed me!" I exclaimed, coming back into the kitchen with all the drama of a Bennett sister.

Nana clapped her hands together as I sat down, my lips still warm with the memory of what had happened.

Campbell Maclean had kissed me!

"My plan worked then," Nana said.

I looked up from the slump I had fallen into on the table.

"What does that mean, Nana?" I narrowed my eyes, she *had* done it on purpose.

"Nothing," She waved her hand around the kitchen to nothing in particular. "Just something from one of my magazines."

I looked at Nana who had gone back to reading. Poor Johnny, Nana hadn't thought much of him. I felt the urge to talk to my Mum, and I needed to speak to Mairi. And soon.

"At least now you don't have to choose," Nana went on. "In my day, you had one person and one person only, none of these modern options." She brushed invisible crumbs from the table.

"I disagree, Nana. It's nice to have choices." I rested my head on the table, as though it had suddenly grown unbearably heavy with the weight of emotion.

"I've read about it, Isla, it only complicates things, best to have a clean slate," Nana said, getting up from the table with the teapot. She took it to the sink and started rinsing it.

I raised my head and pouted with the exertion of it all. "Well, currently I don't have anything."

"You're wrong, Isla," Nana said, boiling the kettle. "You have the world at your feet." Nana was in a very good mood. I, on the other hand, had gone to bed later that night and slept fitfully.

I thought the days and nights I'd been daydreaming of Campbell Maclean were behind me.

Until that kiss.

Now I didn't know what I felt again and while I was toying with my feelings about Campbell, I had given Johnny the wrong impression. I groaned.

I sent a text to Mairi. I needed her now.

EMERGENCY TRIP. I hoped the capital letters conveyed the urgency of the situation.

My phone pinged.

Tonight x

I sighed with relief. She would be here tonight. Just knowing that made things feel better. I could keep everything together until Mairi arrived, and then I would let myself fall apart.

I swung my feet out of bed. Time to get ready for the day. I had made a commitment to my family and that came first — with Sea Colme Cottage to run, my love life would have to wait.

Moments later I was in the kitchen, Charlie at my heels.

"Ready for business!" I announced.

Nana was filling the teapot and Loretta had just finished spooning baked beans onto two plates.

"I'll take those in," I said. I picked the plates up and made my way out of the kitchen.

"You're chirpy this morning," Loretta said, a trace of a smile teasing the edge of her lips

I nodded, avoiding Nana's gaze.

"Lass has the world at her feet," I heard Nana saying as I walked out. I looked at my feet, but nothing. Just as I expected.

The morning passed in a blur. With the computer back up and running the checkouts had gone smoothly. I wanted to text Johnny again to let him know how grateful I was. I stopped myself, reasoning that if he hadn't replied to the last two messages, he was even less likely to reply to a third.

After all the guests had checked out I sat at the reception desk to go through the emails, with a notepad in case any immediate tasks needed doing, and braced myself for whatever the inbox held. I logged in and watched the spinning wheel with peeled-back eyes.

Nothing.

I clicked it again and waited patiently while it spun.

Still nothing.

I refreshed the whole page, hoping that would help. Nothing happened. No new emails and no existing chains of messages were updated. It was all very strange.

Instinctively I reached for my phone, I needed Johnny's help. I swiped open the phone and scrolled to his number. I hesitated to make the call. I looked at the email inbox and Johnny's number.

I couldn't do it, not after Nana's meddling. I needed to apologise face to face.

Thankfully there was still time left before mum and dad returned to sort out any hiccups and Mairi was arriving later — she might be able to help with my IT issues as much as my emotional ones.

I closed the laptop and went into the kitchen. Nana and Loretta were sitting at the table.

"How were the rooms, Loretta?" I asked. I'd heard mum and dad ask the same thing, every day, for as long as I could remember.

"Oh fine, Isla. The guests never make too much of a mess."

I was glad about it. At least something in this place was doing what it was supposed to.

"I'm having another cuppa, then it's time to start the scones." Nana got to her feet and began refilling the kettle. Scones already! The day was passing quickly, I'd have time to take Charlie for a long walk this afternoon before check-in started.

"No time like the present," I said, with as much cheerfulness as I could muster and set to work.

As I mixed the cold butter and flour between my fingers to make the sand-like texture needed for scones, I thought of my hands in Campbell's hair. I took a deep breath. I'd heard nothing from him and had no way of contacting him, as he'd never texted me his number. The only option I had was to do what he did and turn up unannounced at his door. Not that I knew where he lived.

Maybe it was better that way. After what he'd said about loving my hair, I couldn't be trusted not to blurt out that I loved him and had had a crush on him ever since I'd started work at JD Banff and Partners. I still had little idea what impact that moment in the corridor was going to have.

I know mum loved dad, and Nana loved grandpa, but had they had moments of passion? Had they always known they would choose each other?

There were so many questions I had. I looked up from the mixing bowl. Nana and Loretta were idling at the table, and I was glad that my thoughts were private.

Every time I thought of Campbell, I couldn't help but feel guilty about Johnny. I hoped he would reply to my messages soon. I needed to know that he was okay.

I shaped the scone dough into rounds and dusted my hands with flour. If making scones came naturally to me, why couldn't love? I looked over at the kitchen clock — in three hours Mairi would be here and we could make sense of the mess. I set the shaped mounds on a greased baking tray.

"That's the scones done!"

I walked with the tray to the oven. Nana had pre-heated it for me, and I slotted the scones onto a middle shelf.

"I might have a coffee," I said.

Nana looked up from her newspaper.

"There's some in the cupboard love."

I took my apron off and hooked it to the back of the kitchen door.

"I think I need a *frothy* coffee," I said. "There's a new coffee shop on the High Street that I'd noticed when I was walking with Campbell. I'll take Charlie along and introduce myself. They might want to be part of the Christmas market." I looked at Charlie who had sat up in his basket.

"Besides I'm sure Charlie will enjoy the walk as much as me, won't you boy?"

I patted my thigh and Charlie leapt out of his bed to my side.

As I put on my jacket I shook away any possibility that I was taking a walk to *that* coffee shop on the off chance I might bump into Johnny.

Charlie loved sniffing the air along the High Street, especially near the bakers. I waved to Joyce as we passed — she had worked behind the counter there since I'd been at primary school and always gave me a cheerful smile. The bakery stall at the Christmas market was always well-stocked with goodies. At Christmas, they made Scandinavian treats of lebkuchen biscuits and cute gingerbread house decorating kits. Dad was partial to their raspberry jam Linzer biscuits and we were all fans of Joyce's secret sinful Christmas loaf cake, and Joyce always made sure to put a bag of goodies aside for us.

As I walked along I mentally checked the stall holders off from memory as I passed by their premises — there was Goszia in the gift shop, Angela in the Wool shop, Katie in the florist, Delia from the womenswear shop, Seb and Sally from the toy shop, Gita in the eco store, and Marty from the newsagents. I stopped outside the Italian restaurant and the memory of Campbell offering to take us to lunch there popped back into my mind. It was a memory that made me feel warm inside, and I looked through the darkened windows, imagining us holding hands over a glass of wine, some delicious pasta, and bowls of tiramisu.

No! I stopped that train of thought — I was worse than Nana with my romantic notions. There hadn't been another firm invitation with a date or time attached to it, so it didn't count. I had no idea when I'd see Campbell again. Charlie pulled me along the High Street until we reached the new coffee shop, Java Lava. As I tied Charlie up outside, the door opened and the woman with pink hair that I'd met with Johnny leaned halfway out.

"Bring him in!" she said. "We're dog-friendly!"

18

Java Lava's interior was gorgeous. I knew Mum would adore its muted shades of green and grey, the low chairs. Its ethos echoed that of Sea Colme Cottage. If I didn't know better, I'd have sworn mum had designed it! Had she been branching out with a side hustle behind our backs?!

The tables were full of trendy people tapping away at laptops.

"What a gorgeous pup!" The woman with pink hair who'd ushered us in was smiling at Charlie.

"Thanks," I said, and looked down at Charlie. He was looking particularly cute today, his hair flopping into his eyes.

"Is he allowed a treat?"

"Of course!" I appreciated her asking me first. "But be warned, you'll make a friend for life!" I chuckled.

She knelt down to feed Charlie the treat.

"What a friend to make!" She ruffled his neck and stood up.

"Hello, again, Isla isn't it?" She offered her hand, her nails the same shade of pink as her hair.

"Yes, and you're Sally? And this is Charlie," I said. "You've done an amazing job with this place." I looked around the walls, taking in more of the interior decor.

"Thanks, it was all my boyfriend, Caleb. His handiwork. We're so pleased with it."

"It looks brilliant." I smiled at her. "My parents run Sea Colme Cottage, the B&B. You must pop by to say hello." I gestured around the cafe. "Mum will love what you've done with the place."

"Jan and Dave?" she said. "We met them already — in fact, we have them to thank for inspiring us to move here and set up the business."

I wasn't surprised, I'd heard lots of stories like this throughout my lifetime. Mum and dad were well-loved and respected in the town. That's probably why I loved it here so much. Everywhere I went, I knew everyone and they knew me. Mairi sometimes said she found it claustrophobic, but I found it reassuring. If I was being truthful, I'd only moved to Edinburgh after university to please Tim and be closer to Mairi. If Tim had wanted to set up a home in North Berwick I'd have been delighted. The commute to Edinburgh wasn't too long after all. It would have been nice to come home 'home' after work every day. Maybe then I wouldn't have disliked my job at JD Banff so much.

"I'm guessing mum has told you all about the Christmas market?"

Sally made her way back around the counter. "She has, although I haven't had confirmation yet about our stall. We don't want to clash with anyone else."

My face fell.

"Oh gosh, sorry, Sally. I'm supposed to be checking on emails while they're away but I've hit a bit of an issue. Technical stuff…"

Sally looked concerned. "Why don't I make you a coffee and we can have a chat? I might be able to help."

Sally looked friendly, and I did need help with the market and the emails. It would be good to chat it over with someone other than Nana.

"Take a seat and I'll be right with you. Caleb can run the ship for a bit," Sally said.

I made my way over to a table in the corner, and Charlie settled at my feet while I shook myself out of my coat, appreciating the warmth of the cafe. The air definitely had more chill in it now. Winter wouldn't be too far away. Soon I'd be wearing my hat and scarf for protection from the harsh wind which gusted in off the sea.

"I have to say, and you probably hear it all the time, but you look exactly like your mum." Sally arrived at the table and placed a tray laden with coffee, mugs and some delicious-looking cakes.

I smiled. "Apart from the hair, right?" I hadn't been gifted with mum's ultra-sleek hair. Instead, I had dad's unruly spray of brown curls.

"You have great hair," Sally said, taking a seat. "I'd kill for curls like that."

I smiled. I liked my curls, although I could never control them.

"I wish I was brave enough to try a colour like that," I said, looking at her pink bob.

Sally's hair was bright pink, like a bowl of strawberry ice cream, but somehow it looked completely natural, suiting her colouring.

"I always go pink for the holiday season," she said. "I'm early this year, but I thought with the cafe opening, I wouldn't have time, so...' She touched her hair and came over a little shy. I liked her immediately.

"It must be hard work here. I'm running Sea Colme while mum and dad are away and it's exhausting! *And* I have help!" I reached for one of the delicious-looking cappuccinos.

Sally took a cup herself and looked around the cafe.

"We're so excited to be up and running, I think we're running on adrenaline alone." She giggled.

"So the business is yours and Caleb's?" I asked picking up a teaspoon to feed myself the frothy milk from the cappuccino. My favourite part.

"Yes, and a lot of help from friends and our parents."

"What made you choose here?" I asked, it was obvious they were not from here.

"Our friends, Johnny and Katie, moved here during the lockdown. We came to visit them when things started opening back up and we fell in love with the place. We'd always spoken about giving up our jobs and running a business and then when Johnny said this unit was up for lease, we decided..." Sally stopped speaking and looked at me.

I had the teaspoon full of frothy coffee halfway to my lips.

"What is it?" Sally seemed concerned.

"Do you know Johnny well?" I put the spoon back on the tray.

Sally smiled and nodded. "Yes, he's Caleb's best friend." She clapped her hands together. " Of course, you would have caught his eye!"

I gulped.

"Would I?" I said. The thought made my pulse quicken.

"You both have dogs!" Sally said, stating the more obvious reason why we would have met.

"Ahhh," I said, with relief. "Pickles!"

"Pickles is a cutie," Sally said, oblivious to my discomfort.

"She is, Charlie and her play well." I sipped my coffee. "And er, Johnny is rather lovely. He fixed my laptop." Was I babbling? I couldn't tell.

"He's such a nice guy," Sally said. "Which is why it's so nice to see him out and about. I don't mean to be presumptuous but I was delighted to see him with you last week. It was awful with what happened with him and Katie, he's taken it hard." Sally said a little sadly.

I nodded.

"I recently split up with my boyfriend, and it hasn't been the easiest of times, I dread to think what it's like when it's not amicable."

Sally looked into her coffee cup.

"Well, it wasn't exactly amicable with Johnny and Katie," she said quietly.

"Oh?" I said, picking up my coffee cup. I'd missed this kind of thing with Mairi. We used to have a little gossip now and again, always harmless, but enjoyable all the same.

Sally wrinkled her nose. "It's not a secret, so I'm not betraying anyone's trust. I'm not that sort of person." She lifted her chin into the air and I liked her even more.

I nodded and willed her to continue. "Me neither." I wanted to know the gossip about Johnny's relationship. Salacious or not.

Sally leaned in and whispered.

"She cheated on him."

I sat back in my chair, my mouth part open in shock.

"No," I said softly.

Sally nodded her head glumly.

"Some guy at work. Poor Johnny. He adored her, so naturally, he was devastated. Now we worry that it will ruin his trust in people."

I shrank into my chair a little. Just yesterday Johnny, who I had almost kissed on the beach, had caught me and Campbell kissing in the kitchen. No wonder he wasn't answering my texts. I didn't blame him one bit.

"Gosh," I said to Sally. "Poor Johnny."

I wondered if I should tell her what had happened. Who better to give me some clarity about Johnny and the situation with Campbell?

"Actually," I began, just as Caleb called her from behind the counter.

"Hold that thought," Sally said and made her way to help with the queue that had started to form.

I ruffled Charlie's fur and sipped my cappuccino, helping myself to a bite of cake. Both were delicious. Sally and Caleb must have a stall at the Christmas Market! I needed to get onto those emails.

"Sorry, Isla…" Sally came past with a tray, laden with empty cups and crumpled napkins. "It looks like it's going to continue like this for a bit longer. I need to help out." Sally's cheeks were flushed, and the noise in the cafe was rising with the lunchtime crowd.

"Of course! Don't worry, I do need to walk Charlie and get back to Nana. It was lovely meeting you."

I started to collect my things and went to pay for the coffee.

"First one is on the house!" Sally beamed. "It was lovely to chat with you, perhaps we can do this again? I don't know many people here." I liked her openness, tinged with a hint of shyness.

Mairi would like Sally too, I knew it. I imagined the three of us walking on the beach together. It would be nice to have a group of friends down here. I hadn't settled in Edinburgh and Mairi was my only friend, mainly because I'd spent all my time with Tim. I needed to branch out and make new friends. Plus, new friends who could explain to Johnny that I wasn't a harlot would be ideal. I'd like that a lot!

"That would be great," I said. "I'll give you my number and you can text when you get a moment?"

Sally smiled and held out her order pad and pen. "Pop it on there, and I'll text. We can maybe go to Barnacles before the new owner takes over. I've heard it's lovely."

I looked up from scribbling my number on the pad. Barnacles had a new owner?

"Sorry, what did you just say?"

19

The drive over to St Abbs took forty minutes. It was a beautiful coastal town, and if I didn't live in North Berwick, I'd probably live there. It was so pretty it was used in Hollywood films and music videos.

I checked my rearview mirror, where Charlie sat with his tongue lolling out in the back seat, looking his usual happy self. Mum and dad's car was a dream to drive, all plush leather and a camera that helped you park. I smiled despite myself. The laptop was in a bag beside me, I was finally getting the booking system fixed. Time was ticking on, mum and dad would be back in a week, and I still hadn't managed to get into the email account to check the market updates. I had tried resetting the password, but it linked to an account I didn't have access to, so it was useless.

My only option was to take it back to the agent, Wendy, who had signed mum up with the new booking system. She'd been so friendly when I called and assured me she'd fix it in minutes.

I wished mum would call or text. I didn't want to interrupt their break but I needed to speak to her about Barnacles. I'd gone home from Java Lava straight away and told Nana, who had already heard from Loretta. Was I the last person in the town to find out?

Hetty and Burt were finally retiring, and closing the cafe at the end of the month. I knew they were older than the other shopkeepers and restaurant owners, and of course, they deserved to retire, but I had thought they would always be at Barnacles.

It seemed unfair to lose a local institution.

Over the pandemic, a few shopkeepers had sold up and moved away, so it wasn't a surprise. Real estate in the town was snapped up quickly — Sally and Caleb were proof of that. They'd moved fast to secure Java Lava, and it had been a great addition to the high street, so I wasn't opposed to new businesses. Barnacles had a special place in my heart, that was all. I'd grown up there, and it was mine and Mairi's meeting place. I guessed we'd have to find somewhere new.

I pressed the buzzer to Wendy's office and waited with Charlie beside me.

Wendy's office was set above one of the garages close to the harbour. If I had time I would stroll the harbour and a portion of the cliff-top walkway with Charlie, the views were stunning.

I walked up a narrow hallway to be greeted by Wendy at the top of the stairs.

"Hello, thanks for seeing me so soon," I said, taking off my scarf.

"Oh you're your mum's double," she said immediately. "I'd know you anywhere. And this must be the famous Charlie?" Wendy leaned forward to ruffle Charlie behind the ears.

Wendy was a middle-aged woman, with a shock of red hair and a beaming smile. I could see her and mum being instant friends.

"Come on in, and let's get you sorted." Wendy's voice was cheery and capable. I had no doubt she'd be the one to resolve my laptop issues.

"It's been playing up all week. As I said on the phone, I can't access the emails."

I sat in a chair opposite Wendy as she tapped at the keyboard, glasses perched precariously on the end of her nose.

I was mesmerised by her productivity, and could only stare in wonder as she worked. She flicked through a folder of programming commands, rested it on the desk in front of her and traced one finger across the page as she typed with the other hand.

As the minutes slipped by, I stole a look at her desk, strewn with folders. My eyes rested on one with a logo I'd recognised. JD Banff and Partners. Why would Campbell's company have any need of Wendy's services, I wondered? JD Banff was an investment company, with its own IT department and support teams. Mum had said Wendy dealt in hospitality. Maybe it was something to do with an investment they were involved in.

"Ta-dah!" Wendy turned the laptop to face me with a victorious flourish.

I leaned forward and was relieved to see the familiar booking screen up and running.

"I reset the password to the original. You will have the option to change it, so let your mum know." Wendy tapped a few keys and the screen changed from the email account.

"Just click that icon when you're ready to tackle the emails," Wendy said. "It looks like there are a few, that should keep you busy."

I craned my neck to see the email tally in the corner of the screen. One hundred and five! I gulped and felt my face go hot.

All those emails to deal with, and only a week until mum and dad were back — and just two weeks until the Christmas market!

Wendy tapped the laptop and closed it, handing it back across the desk to me.

My eyes flicked to the JD Banff folder.

"I used to work for them," I said, pointing to it.

"Oh," Wendy said. "They're a new client. Quite an exciting little project too."

"Mum said you only do hospitality clients, is that right?" I knew I was prying, but I couldn't help myself.

"That's right," Wendy said with a smile. The conversation was over. "That should be everything," she gestured at the laptop. "But if you need anything from me, don't hesitate to call, okay?"

She smiled at me, and I got the feeling I was being dismissed before I could ask any more questions.

"Will you be at the Christmas Market?" I asked, sure that Mum had already invited her.

"Wouldn't miss it. Any excuse to be festive! It's my favourite time of year." Her smile was huge.

This was why I loved Christmas, it made everyone happy.

I took a quick walk through the harbour and then detoured up to the cliffs, Charlie at my heels. Up here the air was bracing and I looked out to sea, soaking up the mixtures of blues and greys and the miles and miles of the North Sea. Feeling clear-headed, my mind switched from worrying about the multiplicity of emails to the folder on Wendy's desk.

It could be connected to Campbell's freelance project, or the smaller projects he said his dad worked on. But Campbell had asked if I knew anything about hospitality. There had to be a link.

I put the worry aside, I had more immediate concerns to think about.

It was Friday and that meant Sea Colme had more check-ins than usual. Loretta always took a half day so she could be at home to look after her grandchildren. It would be down to Nana and me to run things. With that thought in mind, I called Charlie to heel and made my way back to the car.

Everything was fine at the B&B, guests had checked out with no problems, and Nana had made the scones before 'going for a read'. So I immediately re-leashed Charlie and made my way to Java Lava. The inside of the coffee shop was a riot of festive colour. Greens, golds, reds, silver, no colour had been left out from Sally's decorations. A small traditional-looking Santa stood at the door, rimmed glass on his nose, holding a sign wishing all customers a Happy Holiday in one hand and a coffee cup in the other.

"Isla!" Sally called from behind the counter. It was nice to be welcomed by such a cheery voice. "What can I get you?"

I ordered a coffee. "The place looks amazing, so Christmassy!" I gushed.

Sally smiled and her cheeks flushed.

I noticed the last time I was there that several people were using the tables as workstations, and I thought it would be a good place to work through the emails.

I held up the laptop in my hand.

"I've finally got my laptop fixed, so I'm here to work if you don't mind?"

I settled at a table by the window and took my laptop out, ready to tackle the dreaded emails.

"Here you go!" Sally set a coffee tray down in front of me. "I won't disturb you while you're working, but pop over if you want a chat."

As I logged into the booking system and manoeuvred to the email tab, I noticed that the email tally had risen to a hundred and thirty.

I swallowed and clicked on the tab, and watched as the emails downloaded from the main server.

I started at the bottom, checking the earliest emails. I sipped my coffee and tapped out replies, appreciative of the cheery atmosphere of the cafe.

Most messages were stallholders checking in with mum. A few of the names were unfamiliar to me, and I calculated that we'd have five new stalls. Java Lava was on the list, as well as a few local people who had set up online shops during the pandemic. One thing was for sure, visitors would not be short of Christmas gift ideas.

I smiled at the laptop, pleased with myself. I'd been worrying unnecessarily, just as mum had said. Finishing the replies, I had a few minutes to chat with Sally before I needed to head back to Sea Colme to check new guests in. I took my empty cup over to the counter.

"Did you get everything done?" Sally indicated the laptop.

"Thankfully!" I said. "Mum told me not to worry and she meant it. The market is going to be even more awesome than ever this year!"

"We're looking forward to it. Your mum seems very capable," Sally said.

I turned to look out of the window. A flash of movement across at Barnacles caught my attention and I moved forward to get a better look. I stopped in my tracks.

"Are you okay?" Sally sounded concerned for me. "You look like you've seen a ghost."

It wasn't a ghost. It was someone very much alive. Someone who should have been a million miles away in Edinburgh.

20

Sally had come around the counter to stare out of the window with me. "*Who* is she?"

"Sophie Cannon," I said, spitting out the name of my former manager.

"Yes, but who *is* she?!" Sally chuckled.

"I used to work with her, she was awful" I couldn't believe she was here and going into Barnacles.

I shook my head.

It felt unreal.

Sophie Cannon had made my life unpleasant for months. All the hopes I'd had for my new job at JD Banff and Partners were dashed by her treatment of me.

"She doesn't look very friendly," Sally said, and I wanted to hug her for being so perceptive.

"She isn't," I confirmed.

"You don't think she's the new owner do you?" Sally spoke the fear that had been crashing around my head.

"I hope not." I turned away from the window. I needed to get back to Sea Colme.

"Do you want me to walk back with you?" Sally asked.

I was touched by her warmth, it was exactly the sort of thing Mairi would do.

"Don't be silly, you have a business to run! I promise my life isn't this complicated usually." I attempted a laugh.

"Life is life," Sally said wisely, shrugging.

I zipped up my coat and followed in Charlie's wake as he led the way back to Sea Colme Cottage. Every inch of me was on high alert. I needed answers. Was this connected to the folder on Wendy's desk? Why hadn't

Campbell said anything about it? He'd been to visit us twice now. I was angry at the thought that he knew more than he had told me. He knew Sophie had been a big part of the reason that I didn't want to work at his father's company, and I had told him how much I loved this town — why wouldn't he have said something about Sophie taking over a business here? It was inexcusable.

It felt like my North Berwick dream was turning into a nightmare. I loved this town, loved it with every inch of my soul, and I did not want to have to share any part of it with Sophie Cannon.

The next morning, the breakfast shift went by quickly and soon I was loading the dishwasher with the dirty dishes.

"Are you sure you don't mind, Nana?" I asked for the third time.

"Lass, how many times do I need to tell you? He'll be fine with me! As long as you give him a good walk this morning, he'll spend the afternoon snoozing with me in the conservatory."

I rarely left Charlie, and never with Nana, but today I had no choice. I had no one else to rely on and I needed to do the unthinkable and go to get answers from Campbell.

"You could just email him" Nana called from the sink where she was filling the kettle. "You have access to his email address now."

"I know." I sighed. I couldn't explain why I needed to speak to Campbell face to face. Some things needed to be said in person, rather than via a machine.

I took Charlie for a long walk on the beach, throwing sticks and watching him chase them. Out here on the beach, with the November wind whipping my hair, nothing seemed to matter. It all seemed irrelevant. But it was a feeling I knew I couldn't hold on to, and as soon as I was back in the town, my fears of bumping into Sophie would come rushing back. I thought about Johnny, and falling onto the sand with him. I wasn't surprised he hadn't texted me back, and I hoped he was okay.

If I saw him now, I'd tell him he had nothing to worry about with Campbell. I was so angry with Campbell, and my anger spurred me on to take Charlie back to Nana and head for the train. If I was going to the offices, my usual beach attire of jeans, trainers and a sweater was too casual. I'd opted for my smarter black leather boots so I could tuck my jeans into them, and a shirt. I looked country casual now, instead of beach-ready. Before I knew it the train had arrived at Edinburgh Waverley, and I was weaving my way through the crowds towards the exit. I realised I hadn't thought of stopping by my flat, which was all the proof I needed that I'd mentally left Edinburgh and moved back home.

Mairi was waiting for me outside her office, as we'd arranged, and she walked with me toward JD Banff and Partners premises on George Street. She'd insisted on accompanying me for moral support.

"I can't believe he wouldn't have told you about Sophie," she was saying as we walked along the street.

I grabbed Mairi's arm and dragged us into an empty doorway.

"What is it?' She peered out.

"It's Campbell!" I said, my voice barely a whisper. My eyes couldn't believe what I was seeing.

Campbell was walking out of the building with Sophie, and they were chatting and laughing together. *Chatting*! And *laughing*! That wasn't the Campbell and Sophie I remembered. They'd barely spoken out with work meetings when I'd been on the payroll. What had happened in the weeks since I'd left?

"We should march over there and confront them," Mairi said, moving forward with purpose. I appreciated her desire to stand with me in this fight, but I reached my arm out to stop her.

"No," I said, deflated.

"Why not?" She questioned. "They are *right there*." She pointed across the street.

I shook my head.

"It doesn't matter, look at them. That's not the way I remember them, they barely spoke to each other when I worked there."

"Oh," Mairi said, understanding. "Looks like they're good friends now..."

I nodded. We both watched as Campbell and Sophie stood in the street laughing, Sophie's hand on Campbell's arm. He did not attempt to move it.

"He used me," I said as realisation dawned on me. Of course, Campbell would be with someone like Sophie, I'd known it all along. "This was another one of my romantic notions, like mine and Tim's relationship. It wasn't real."

"Come on," Mairi said, jostling me onwards. "John Lewis has the best decorations. That will cheer you up, and there's a new ramen place opened in the St James Quarter."

As I let Mairi lead me away, tears sprang to my eyes. I'd thought the situation with Campbell had all been a dream, and now I had concrete proof that it was. I still had no idea why he'd kissed me, or why he'd kept the secret about Barnacles. Maybe he'd wanted some inside information? I thought of us walking the high street and me telling him about all of the businesses and their owners. Was he just using me to further a business deal?

I knew one thing for sure: girls like Sophie were his type, not girls like me. I had been a fool to think it was anything else.

Mairi was right, the decorations in John Lewis did cheer me up, and as we wandered around I felt like my trip hadn't been wasted. It was lovely spending some time with her. We ate ramen at the new bar, which was delicious, and before I knew it, Mairi's lunch hour was over and I was on the train home. I hadn't got the answers I'd wanted, but no answers were still answers, in a way, I guessed.

With my silly notions of romance with Campbell out of the picture, I could get back to my original plan of motivating Mairi to move back to North Berwick and write my book.

I stared out of the window, imagining the two of us with our future husbands, having a picnic on the beach. As the train neared my stop I felt my body relax, and I stepped off the train with a slight smile.

"Isla!" Loretta's voice called to me across the platform.

My whole body tensed and panic rose in my chest.

"What's happened?" I said. "Is Charlie okay?"

Loretta shook her head. "Charlie is fine. It's your Nana."

And at that moment, it felt like my world began to collapse around me.

21

Nana looked much smaller and frail than usual, her head resting in the crisp cotton-covered hospital pillows. Her arms lay on either side of her body on top of the cover, and wires and tubes connected her to machines that bleeped beside her. I sat in the only available chair, holding her hand. I told her over and over again that I was sorry I had left her. The tears that had streamed down my face earlier had dried.

Going all the way to Edinburgh to try to confront Campbell felt ridiculously stupid now. Who cared if Sophie took over Barnacles? All that mattered was Nana was okay. I looked up from the bed briefly and gazed around the room.

The nurses had tried to bring some seasonal cheer to patients — Nana's bed had tinsel woven through the headboard, and the windows had colourful twinkle lights around them. Nana was like mum and me. She loved Christmas, but I knew she'd especially love the tinsel. She always said tinsel smelled like Christmas, and although when I was a child I didn't understand what she meant by that, as I'd grown older I couldn't resist smelling tinsel and finally understood what she meant. That dusty, metallic smell *was* as Christmassy as cinnamon and oranges, popcorn and roast turkey. My stomach lurched when I thought ahead to Christmas this year. Would we be crowded around this hospital bed? Forced to be cheery as we worried about Nana's health?

I felt a hand on my shoulder and turned my head to see Mairi.

"I came as soon as I could," she whispered.

"Oh Mairi," I stood up and we hugged. She rubbed my back and I cried into her shoulder.

"I can't lose my Nana," I said

"It's okay, she'll be fine. It was a fall, the doctors said."

I shook my head.

"I left her behind with Charlie, I shouldn't have."

I looked back at Nana, asleep in bed. "This is my fault," I whispered, tears streaming down my face.

"Don't be hard on yourself, Isla. Older people fall all the time."

"Mum asked me to watch her," I said, determined not to listen.

"Good luck watching your Nana! She runs circles around you all!" Mairi rested her hands on the back of the chair. "Have you spoken to your mum?"

I shook my head.

"Despite everything, Nana would go mad if I stopped their holiday. They only have two days left."

I sat back on the chair and picked up Nana's hand, giving it a gentle squeeze.

"You better not tell your mum," Nana said. Mairi and I gasped. It was quiet, and her throat sounded dry, but her voice was as clear as a bell.

"Nana!" I cried, tears streaming down my face. "You're awake!"

"You're not getting rid of me yet, lass," she said, opening her eyes.

"Good to see you awake, Nana," Mairi said from behind me.

As Mairi left the room to fetch a nurse, Nana squeezed my hand gently.

"And you're not to get yourself all worked up about this, you hear me?"

"I shouldn't have left you," I shook my head. "I should have — "

Nana interrupted me. "Stop it, Isla. Please." She shifted her frail frame in the bed and stuck her chin in the air. "It's not my first fall."

"Nana, mum has been so worried." I gave her hand a gentle squeeze.

Nana moved her hand to place it on top of mine.

"I'm her mother," she said. "It's *my* place to worry about her, not the other way around."

She patted my hand gently. I looked into her eyes, seeing Nana in a different light.

"I understand that," I nodded. "But you've given us a bit of a fright." I couldn't help but press my point. Nana was older, she should be slowing down a little.

"Listen, Isla. When it's our time, it's our time and there's nothing we can do about it. Look at your Grandpa, we didn't know he'd be gone so soon." She seemed to be welling up at the memory. "Every day is a blessing, and I enjoy every single one. I love my family. I'm the luckiest woman in North Berwick."

A single tear trickled down Nana's cheek. I pulled a fresh tissue out of the pack to wipe it away gently.

Mairi came back into the room, followed by a young nurse.

"Hello, Mabel," she said in brisk tones. "Nice of you to join us!" She took a clipboard from the foot of Nana's bed and turned to me and Mairi. "Why don't you two go and get a coffee while I have a chat with Mabel?"

Mairi and I stood in the hallway, peering back into the room as the nurse sat down on Nana's bed.

"Thank god she's okay," Mairi said.

I nodded and wiped my nose with a tissue. Mairi led me away from Nana's door, her arm around my shoulder.

We took seats at the end of the corridor and Mairi let me cry it out. Eventually, my tears stopped, and I wiped the last of them away with my tissue.

"When are you moving back ?" Mairi asked.

I looked at her through my red-rimmed eyes.

"What makes you think I'm moving back?"

"Well, you have a flat, you'll need to move back eventually." Mairi looked at me and I realised I had misunderstood her. She had meant when was I moving back to Edinburgh.

I exhaled, feeling like I'd been holding that breath for the last few weeks.

"I'm not sure, I should be close to Nana for a bit," I said. "Give mum and dad some help while she recovers."

"Of course," Mairi nodded. "It's the right thing to do."

I rested my head on Mairi's shoulder. The nurse came along the corridor.

"The good news is there's nothing broken, just some bruises and a big dent in her pride." She smiled reassuringly. "She should rest up here tonight, but she'll be okay to come home tomorrow."

Mairi and I sighed with relief.

"But has she told you she needs a hip replacement?"

Mairi and I looked at each other. I shook my head.

"No, she hasn't said."

The nurse nodded. "I suspected as much. She's been advised by her doctor, but it's in her notes that she is refusing. Unless and until she has that operation there's a risk she'll keep falling over. So far, she'd been lucky to not sustain any real damage. But…"

The nurse left the words hanging in the air.

"Don't worry, we'll convince her," I said, as Mairi nodded vigorously beside me.

"Pop in to say good night," the nurse suggested, "then let her rest. We'll phone you when she is ready to be discharged tomorrow."

Back in Nana's room, she looked a little sheepish. There would be time to convince her to get the hip replacement once mum and dad were back home. Until then, I was just glad she was okay. I leaned over the bed and breathed in her usual lemon cologne smell.

"Night, night, Nana," I said, planting a kiss on her forehead.

"Night, lass."

"Night Nana," Mairi said, leaning over to kiss Nana's cheek.

"Look after each other, girls," Nana called.

"We will," We both said in unison.

"Oh, Isla," Nana called from the bed as we were almost out of the door. "Campbell called."

I spun around on my heels.

"He did?" My heart raced despite my earlier promises to myself that it didn't matter.

"He said he'd try again, but there was a work project, and he hoped you would be excited." Nana gave a little chuckle.

I pursed my lips. He wanted me to be excited. Did he indeed? I wouldn't upset Nana by telling her the truth about Campbell Maclean, instead, I smiled and nodded.

"Thanks, Nana. Night, night."

As soon as we were far enough away from Nana's room, Mairi turned to me.

"Well?"

"Well, what?"

"You know what. He called you." She stood in front of me, and I tried to sidestep her. "Isla, talk to me," she said, taking hold of my arms so I couldn't move.

"Honestly, Mairi, it's nothing. I have to put this Campbell nonsense out of my mind. You saw them together today and all these comings and goings, surprise visits. All it's done is distract me."

I looked back towards Nana's room.

"Besides, I should be writing. I came here to focus on that."

Mairi rubbed my arms and nodded.

"Come on, let's go to Barnacles and get a drink. We won't be able to do that for much longer."

I shook my head.

"I really should get back to Charlie."

"This Friday, then — your mum and dad will be back by then, right?"

I had no choice but to agree, although the last place I wanted to be was Barnacles.

"Maybe we could go to Luciano's instead?" I said, moving to link arms with her.

"Mmmmm… pasta!" She said, making me giggle.

Back home I thanked Loretta for staying on to watch Charlie — never really part of her job description — and to hold the reins at the B&B.

"Is it just me," Loretta said, "or does it feel like it's been a long month?"

I couldn't disagree.

"It's not just you," I assured her.

"Poor Nana," Loretta said when I told her about the new hip Nana needed and was avoiding. "Ageing. On women, it's much more unfair than on men. Men get sports cars, women get menopause." Loretta raised her eyes to the ceiling.

I smiled.

"Do you want some tea?"

Loretta shook her head.

"No, I'll head back to Pete." She came over and kissed me gently on the cheek. "You've done a really good job, Isla. They'll be proud of you."

I was so touched.

"Thank you, Loretta. But you did most of the heavy lifting, it was a team effort."

I couldn't take credit for all the hard work that went into running this business, and the daily enthusiasm that Loretta showed up to work with every morning. She waved as she left the kitchen and I waited for the front door to shut. Then I walked through to lock it for the night and traipsed upstairs with Charlie, a glass of cold tap water in my hand.

The beach looked eerily pretty at night, shadows strewn from the walkway street lamps. If you looked closely, you could see the sand being whisked up in the wind. I looked up into the night sky at the stars and thought of what Nana had said. She felt like the luckiest woman in North Berwick. I smiled.

Nana was the heartbeat of our family, and with her at the centre, I would get through anything. Even Sophie Cannon running Barnacles.

I fell into bed with a strange sense of optimism.

It was time to forget Campbell Maclean and all of the romantic notions that came with him. And Johnny, too.

I'd take a leaf out of Nana's book and celebrate all of life's little wins, and give thanks for all that I had, instead of what I didn't. Because I had a lot.

I wriggled my toes in the bed to rest beside Charlie's warm body, and before I knew it I was fast asleep. The two of us snored gently, not a care in the world.

22

I had never been more pleased to see mum and dad in my whole life. Charlie and I stood in the dining room window with Nana, watching their taxi pull up, and when the doors opened a sense of relief washed over me. Nana leaned on the stick the hospital had given her, and we looked at each other, giving each other a knowing look.

As I waved to my smiling mum, I gave a huge, thankful sigh and then Nana and I walked to the front door to greet them properly, Charlie at our heels yapping and jumping in excitement.

They were full of chatter and excitement about their trip, and we went straight to the kitchen, where I put on the kettle.

"The sunsets, Isla!" mum said, her eyes all misty as she reminisced. "They were beautiful weren't they, Dave?"

"Spectacular!" Dad agreed. "And the lakes and mountains…" He shook his head. "Unbelievable!"

They brought their tablet out to show us the photos they had taken and we oohed and ahhed through the exhibition.

Mum and dad looked years younger, their faces refreshed, so distinct from the faded couple who had left a month ago. Strange that I never noticed the impact of the weariness that came from running the B&B until it wasn't there.

"It looks beautiful," I said as they flicked through the photo carousel.

Mum and dad turned to look at me and Nana.

"It was, and we can't thank you both enough for giving us this precious opportunity. We really wouldn't have been able to experience it without your help."

Mum's eyes looked teary. She knew better than anyone not to fuss over Nana, but her tears said it all. She had seen the walking stick and was worried.

"I expect you handled everything brilliantly," dad chimed in, attempting to lighten the mood.

Nana and I looked at each other and smiled.

"I think I can speak for the two of us," I said, "when I say we have a renewed appreciation for all the hard work you do."

Dad squeezed mum by the shoulder and they shared a look.

"Well, while we were away, we were thinking we should make more time for things like that, and slow down a little," dad said, turning to me. "Did you enjoy it enough to consider staying on?"

I was speechless. I thought they'd be glad to be back and grab the reins of their business — but the trip seemed to have the opposite effect. They wanted more time! I thought about everything that had happened in the last month, and all the work that had gone into Sea Colme Cottage, the worry that I was doing things wrong, and would ruin things for mum and dad, and it all faded away. None of it mattered, all that worrying had been for nothing. Sea Colme Cottage had almost run itself, I realised.

"I'd be honoured if you wanted me to take this place on," I said with a smile. "But," I added, looking at Nana with uncertainty, "I hope your next trip isn't for a while?"

"No," mum said, chuckling. "We have the Christmas Market to deal with first!" A huge smile spread over her face.

"I had been thinking about moving back permanently," I said, tentatively sharing the thought I'd been having.

"About time!" Nana exclaimed, and mum and dad shared another look.

"We'd hoped you would, but we didn't want to push you," dad said, his hand entwined with mums.

I looked at mum, who smiled.

"I'd love to have you around," mum said. "You're a great help, and maybe you could do some writing here?"

"I have been writing," I announced, feeling good about the work I'd produced over the last few weeks.

The look of joy on my Mum's face was priceless.

"I've started work on a book set here, in North Berwick."

"That's wonderful," mum said, clapping her hands together.

"There's certainly lots of stories to tell here," dad suggested. "You could start a series!"

We all laughed and a warm feeling enveloped me. My family were back together and everything was going to be okay.

"Right," dad said, getting to his feet and gathering our empty mugs. "Who wants another cuppa?"

I looked at Charlie in his basket, tongue lolling out of his mouth.

"I'd better see to Charlie first," I said.

I slipped out of the kitchen with Charlie as they all settled into their second cup of tea, and headed for a walk on the beach.

The air was refreshing as always, and Charlie raced away over the sand before circling back towards me. In the distance, I thought I saw Johnny, but although I craned my neck, I couldn't be sure it was him. He hadn't texted me back, and we hadn't had a chance to meet. I still hoped that might happen in time. I felt embarrassed now about the way things had transpired with Campbell, and I sighed. Love was never easy.

As Charlie ran towards me with a huge and happy smile on his face I wondered how dogs had it all figured out. Have fun, play and stay in the moment — that was a dog's life. How much simpler must life be for them.

I pulled up a chair next to mum as she tapped at the keyboard. It was time to fine-tune the Christmas Market details, and I was honoured she wanted me to be part of the admin effort.

"We're going to have five extra stalls," she said, scanning the screen and writing notes in her blue notebook.

"The trouble that blue notebook gave me when you were away," I muttered, nibbling on a biscuit. I shook my head ruefully.

"Nana told me," mum chuckled. "Sorry love, I did say not to worry."

I hadn't been able to help it. "It must be a Barker trait." I popped the rest of the biscuit in my mouth. It was lovely sitting here with mum. I had missed her so much while she'd been away. We had the table set with biscuits, a pot of tea for her and a coffee press for me.

"Did you know there's a new Italian deli opening?" mum said, still writing notes on her pad. I wondered how she knew but suspected the town's grapevine had been buzzing from the moment she arrived back in town.

I reached for another biscuit. Mum was trying a new recipe and I was the official taste tester — so far I gave them full marks.

"Hetty and Burt were delighted to pass their premises over, and apparently the new owner is lovely."

My stomach dropped. I really should tell mum the whole Campbell and Sophie story, but I couldn't. It seemed so trivial. Besides, if Burt and Hetty had picked Sophie from all the people they could have sold to, she must be a good fit. I decided to leave the story for another day.

"They're going to have a stall at the market," mum continued. "Italian delicacies." She sounded the word out, and I realised she was typing the details into her spreadsheet.

"Doesn't Luciano's already have a stall for Italian stuff?" I didn't like the idea of Sophie muscling in and displacing a local business.

Mum shook her head. "Not for sweet treats. Luciano's makes that wonderful turkey and cranberry pizza, but not sweet treats."

"Ohhh, yes," I said. How could I forget that pizza? It was delicious. Made exclusively for the first Christmas market, it had proven so popular it was now on their Christmas menu every year! My mouth watered at the thought of crispy herby pizza dough, shredded turkey, and sweet cranberry jam.

"I think we're all set," Mum announced, shuffling her notes. "Now I need to get started on the Christmas buns."

My eyes lit up at the sound of Christmas buns.

"We tasted the best buns in Norway," she said, sipping her tea. "They were divine. I was in my element." She exhaled with remembered satisfaction. "Now I need to get back to my pilates class to work them off!"

I scoffed. Mum had the same figure as me. She seemed to mentally appraise me, as I fed another biscuit into my mouth.

"Perhaps you should start coming along too?" she said.

"Mum!"

"Not to lose weight or for fitness," she assured me, putting a hand on my arm. "But for the social side, you know — to meet a few people."

I considered her invitation, looking at the biscuits and deciding not to take another.

"Honestly, it's very social, the studio does *everything* — yoga, meditation, pilates, barre classes. You'd love it!" I must have looked doubtful, because she added, "And it's not only people my age, it's *all* ages."

I could tell Mum was warming to the idea, but I wasn't one for exercise classes. Mairi had tried to get me to join her gym, without success. I preferred walking, and Charlie gave me the perfect excuse for that. I liked being out in the fresh air.

"Maybe if I invited Sally along?" I said, thinking aloud.

Mum scanned her list. "Is that Sally who runs Java Lava?"

I nodded.

"She's lovely, around my age, I think."

"Lovely! Why don't you pop along later and ask her." Mum said, tapping at the keyboard.

"I think Mairi will like her too," I said, conscious of my best friend feeling left out.

I left mum to get started on the Christmas buns and trekked upstairs to my room where my laptop sat, waiting for me to put more words on its screen.

I'd been making great pace on my story and I had found a nice routine of walking Charlie and then settling down to write for a few hours every day. If everything continued according to my plan, I should have a completed manuscript to edit in January. I was delighted at how everything was falling into place.

Despite my reservations about Sophie being in town, I emailed my landlord last week to give notice on my flat in Edinburgh. Dad said he'd drive up with me after the market to collect my things.

It was official, I was making the move back home, and it felt so, so right.

All I had to do was tell Mairi.

23

Mairi had been at my side, one way or another, throughout so many life changes. I was confident that things wouldn't change now, just because I was choosing to move back home.

"I'm glad your Nana is okay," she said as soon as we sat down at Luciano's.

"Thanks," I said. "What a fright she gave us!"

She smiled. "Your Nana is tough."

She was right, Nana *was* tough. And stubborn as an ox, it turned out. None of us could convince her to get the hip operation. Instead, she took the walking stick everywhere she went and said it had helped. That was her code for the matter being settled, and no further discussion would be offered. None of us knew what to do next — it was her decision, and none of us could force her to have an operation she didn't want.

Mairi interrupted my thoughts. "Crazy to think that only a few months ago you were still pinning over Tim."

I scowled at her.

"From this moment forward, all references to Tim are forbidden. He has been *TIM-minated.* I have moved on."

Mairi giggled. Inwardly I was cringing about Tim, it was clear now we were never supposed to be together.

"It was loneliness that I was feeling when I thought I wanted him back," I said. "I realise that now."

Mairi reached a hand across the table to place it over mine.

"I'm happy for you," she said, squeezing my hand. She seemed unusually serious. I took my hand back and she picked up a menu.

"Let's order, I'm starving!"

I looked around the restaurant, noting that Luciano's was quiet for the time of year. With the season over, the place should have been full of locals. I had my usual pang of worry about our small town and hoped Sophie's deli would not be taking customers away from Luciano's.

Right on cue, the doors burst open and a group came in, pushing aside my fears.

The waiter came with table water and breadsticks, and Mairi jerked her head to look past him and I turned my head too and snapped it back immediately.

"What is it?" Mairi asked.

"Johnny," I said with a smile. "Don't look."

How could she not look?! I turned my head slowly too, and there he was, larger than life, sitting in one of the booths, throwing his head back in laughter. I snapped my head back to face Mairi.

She raised her eyebrows.

"I should go and say something," I murmured. I got up to go over to his table.

"No!" Mairi reached across to put her hand on my arm to stop me. I sat back down again.

"Shouldn't I at least say hello? I've sent him messages and had no reply."

Mairi shook her head. "That alone should tell you how he feels. If he hasn't replied, maybe his ego is bruised. He will have seen you. Leave it to him to make contact, if he wants to."

What Mairi was saying made sense. I turned around again to look at Johnny. Our eyes met for a split second, and both of us looked away quickly.

A tiny bubble of anger rose in me, displacing the worry I'd had for him. I hadn't planned for him to see Campbell and me, not at all! And if it had been *me*, I'd have felt terrible — hurt, betrayed, confused, whatever — but I would have replied to a text message, at the very least!

I'd even worried that I'd made him feel less of a part of the community, the worst kind of outsider experience.

"He doesn't look heartbroken," Mairi said, taking a sip of her drink. She made a sour face which I knew had nothing to do with the taste. I couldn't help but sneak another look over my shoulder at Johnny. I noticed Caleb sitting next to him.

How dare he be out having fun, when I had spent the last week imagining him heartbroken at home?!

"At least I can stop feeling bad now." I shrugged. I didn't mean it, I felt terrible, probably worse than before.

"I still can't believe your Nana did that." Mairi giggled. "She is a powerhouse, your Nana. She knows what she wants and gets it, I've always admired that about her."

I hung my head, wishing I was anywhere but here. I didn't like feeling uncomfortable.

"Tell you what, let's get our food to go. We can head to the beach," Mairi suggested, and I nodded.

"Great idea," I said, my voice thick with faux positivity. I gathered up my things and tried not to look in Johnny's direction again.

"Or, actually," Mairi said when we were outside with our warm takeaway bags, "we could go back to your place?"

It was a much better idea, I need the refuge of home. We set off towards the east beach and Sea Colme Cottage.

"How is Charlie getting on with his visits to Tim?" Mairi said it softly, knowing I still wasn't fully on board with the experience.

"It's okay," I admitted. "It's been a great help with Nana recovering. But how do you know if a dog is having fun? It's not like he can tell me."

"I'm sure Charlie would tell you if he wasn't," Mairi said, reassuringly.

I had nothing to worry about. The visits had been going well. I knew Tim would look after him and follow his routine, and Charlie always went away with his tail wagging. It was nice to be in a good place with Tim. It seemed like we had been together in a whole different life, and I felt strange to think I'd ever been reminiscent of days with him. I remembered my Nana saying that sometimes, time needed to pass before you understood why things didn't work out. I understood that now.

"Aside from the dramas of your love life, how has it been, living back here?" Mairi walked in step alongside me.

"Fantastic," I said without an ounce of irony. "I love being away from the city and back beside the sea. And with mum and dad back, it's what I didn't have in Edinburgh." I hadn't yet told Mairi about my intention to stay here, permanently, so I took a deep breath. "I've given up the lease on my flat," I said.

"Really?" Mairi fell silent as we walked.

I sighed. I had hoped to convince her that she should move back too, but I now feared that wasn't an option. I stopped walking and waited as she continued a few steps then turned to look at me. Was it worth one more try?

"Wouldn't you like to be back here too?" I said. "Just like old times?"

She looked uncomfortable and shook her head.

"I'm sorry, Isla, but I couldn't." She looked back towards the high street and then out to sea. What was she seeing? And why couldn't she see what *I* saw?

"Do you like it here?" I didn't understand how Mairi wasn't desperate to be back in our childhood home. She shook her head and let out a sigh.

"It's not enough for me," she said finally. "It never will be."

I couldn't help but feel a little bit wounded.

"I mean it's great for a visit," she added. "But there's nothing here for young people. It's an old person's town."

I felt a pang of something blunt and heavy in my chest. "I'm not an old person," I said indignantly.

"Oh don't get me wrong," she said, reaching out to stroke my arm by way of offering comfort. "I think you fit in here perfectly — you're an old soul, you always have been. But it would be a disaster for me."

"What's that supposed to mean?"

She started to walk on.

"I have different dreams and ambitions," she said, the words drifting on the air.

I couldn't believe what I was hearing, rooted to the spot.

"I have dreams and ambitions!" I said a little louder than I intended. A passing couple looked at me with concern. I hurried to catch up with Mairi.

"Why would you say such a thing?" I felt tears in my eyes. It wasn't like Mairi to say mean things. In all the years we'd been friends, she'd never so much as told me I looked awful — even when I knew I did! "Mairi, what's wrong? Talk to me."

"Nothing," she snapped. "Sometimes it's a bit tedious to hear about your amazing life here and how much you bloody love it."

"You love it here too," I protested. "Or you used to, anyway." What had changed?

"I bloody do not," she snapped.

"You always said you can't wait to move back here when you have children. Didn't you?"

Mairi looked at me and shook her head.

"No, Isla, that's your dream. It's not mine. My dream is to climb the career ladder, I don't want to get married or have children. And I definitely don't want to move back here."

I stared at the stranger standing in front of me. Where had my friend gone and who was this woman, her hair flapping in the evening breeze and her chin jutting out defiantly?

"I thought it was *our* dream," I said, my voice wobbling.

"There's more to life than this town, Isla."

Of course there was! But I liked this town, and I liked the people in it. I cared about the goings on in this town.

"I'm moving away." She blurted out. "There's no easy way to tell you."

I stared at her with an open mouth.

"What?" I whispered.

"From Scotland, from the UK. My company wants me to relocate to Milan. Giles is setting up a new office and he wants me to go with him. I said yes. I leave in two weeks."

She shrugged and looked away.

When I was younger my mum always said the best way to remove a plaster was to rip it straight off. That's what it felt like now. Mairi was tearing off the bandaid, and taking half of my hopes and dreams along with it. I even felt the sting that was left in the aftermath.

We stood staring at each other.

"How long for?"

"Two years." She looked out towards the sea.

I felt my legs weaken and worried I was about to collapse on the sand. I sat down on one of the benches at the edge of the beach. Its plaque said it was for Marvin 'who loved this place'. You and me both, Marvin. But not Mairi. My best friend hates it! So much so, she's leaving the UK.

I felt Mairi sit down beside me but couldn't bring myself to look at her.

"I'm sorry," she said, her voice quiet and sad sounding. "I didn't mean that you don't have dreams and ambitions, I take that back. I don't know where that came from. I think I was too nervous to tell you I was going. I'm sorry."

I looked at her, truly looked at her since she'd arrived that evening. I'd been too caught up in my drama that I hadn't even noticed her. Her hair was shorter, meaning she'd been for a haircut and hadn't told me. That should have been a clue that something had changed. We used to tell each other *everything*.

I felt a stab of shame when I realised I hadn't asked her about her life for so long, instead centring all of our conversations around my problems.

"Mairi, I'm sorry." I turned towards her and let the words hang in the air. "I've been incredibly selfish lately, always talking about the B&B, Campbell, Johnny, Tim, Charlie. I haven't asked about you in ages. I'm a bad friend." I saw a flicker of recognition in her eyes. "I mean it. I'm so sorry." I linked my arm through hers and we sat in silence for a time, both staring out towards the sea, invisible in the darkness.

"Tell me everything," I said finally. "Milan — that sounds amazing..."

She smiled, happiness tinged with sadness, or maybe a creeping finger of fear.

"I'm excited," she confessed.

"You should be!" I said. "I'm excited for you!"

"It is okay for us to want different things in life, Isla," she said and I nodded. Not everyone wanted what I wanted.

"I guess I project my dreams onto everyone," I said.

"We're not all romantics," She smiled.

I gasped in faux horror and put my hands to my cheeks.

"And you're only telling me this now?'

We giggled. Just like old times.

As she talked me through her plans, her ideas, and the opportunities she was hoping for, I fought to keep back tears. My dream of us living in the same village was just that, my dream. But that didn't mean I wasn't happy for her. How could I not be?

I was living my best life, why shouldn't she live hers?

24

On the opening morning of the Christmas Market, Sea Colme Cottage was a hive of activity. Dad was at the beach helping assemble the wooden stall frames, ready for the stallholders to arrive and add their finishing touches. I was at Sea Colme, helping mum and Nana. The kitchen smelled amazing, like Christmas — full of sweet cinnamon, nutmeg, mixed spices and cookie dough. Charlie was at the edge of the table, waiting for scraps, and I had already eaten a good share of mum's Scandinavian cookies and buns.

I dashed into the dining room to collect a box of decorations. I loved helping to decorate mum's stall, and this year she'd brought items from her trip to add. A beautiful blue snow globe, with a chocolate box castle inside and a couple standing in front of it holding hands, would take pride of place as her centrepiece. I gave the globe a little shake and watched as snowflakes whirled around the couple.

Snow was forecast, but we had yet to see a snowflake fall on the beach in all the years the market had been running. Ever hopeful, I was imagining just how magical the place would be if snow were to fall at the Christmas Market.

As I walked over the road to mum's stall, positioned next to dad's BBQ, I gave Sally a wave.

"You're here nice and early!" I said, watching as she weaved tinsel and garlands around the top of her stall.

"I left Caleb and Mary running the shop, and thought I'd get a head start." She smiled. "We haven't seen you in a few days? Is your Nana okay?" Sally's concern was touching, she'd popped around with some cake and flowers for Nana when she'd heard the news of her fall. Mum and dad had been delighted by her thoughtfulness. Now that mum and dad were back, I had taken to writing at the coffee shop and had built up a rapport with Sally. She was so easy to talk to.

"Can you hold onto this for me?" Sally held out a garland, which I took while she got down to reposition her stool. She reached for the garland. Her stall was coffee themed. Tiny coffee cups in every size hung from her garlands — lattes, cappuccinos, flat whites, cold brews, all hand-stitched on felt and attached to a length of material.

"Sally this is wonderful," I breathed.

"Do you think so?" She looked up at me with a huge smile. "I want your Mum to invite us back next year! Caleb and I have been so thankful for her input at Java Lava."

"Oh she adores you, and she's delighted you're willing to accompany her reluctant daughter to yoga!" I laughed.

"I can't wait," Sally said, smiling. Sally had agreed to sign up for yoga classes with me in the new year, and I admired her spirit of joining in and forging community bonds.

Dad wandered over from the other side of the market, a huge Christmas tree in his arms.

"I had better get on with decorating mum's stall," he said.

"You're putting us to shame!" I said to Sally who giggled as I followed dad and his tree.

We got to work untangling lights and garlands and fixing them to the stall the way I had seen mum do over the years. Soon I had warmed up despite the cold weather. Mum and Nana came over to laden the stall with the goodies and we worked as a team, three generations of Barker women, with dad ricocheting between us as we all shouted instructions for him to follow.

"Looking good, ladies!" The voice came from behind us, and although I recognised it, I couldn't immediately put my finger on who it belonged to.

I turned my head slowly, as it dawned on me exactly who had spoken.

There stood a cheery-looking Campbell Maclean.

I froze. Here he was again, turning up unannounced.

"Hi Campbell," Nana said, as Campbell leaned forward to kiss her on the cheek.

"Good to see you up and about, Mabel," he said with a look of concern. How did Campbell know about Nana's fall?

"Nice to see you again, Campbell," mum said, stepping forward to hug him, causing my insides to tumble all over the place.

"Hi Jan, this is better than I imagined. What a great job you have done." Campbell said, causing my mum to blush as she said thank you.

When had mum met Campbell?

I hid behind the counter, pretending to look in the empty box of decorations while I gathered my thoughts.

"Hello Campbell!" dad said, pulling the string of lights on the tree into place. I watched as they shook hands and dad said, "Good to see you again, glad it's going well. Remember we are here if you need us. Now, Jan Nana, is it time for a cuppa?"

"Good idea," mum's tone was strangely high-pitched. "Nana, come on, let's go get the kettle on."

"But I don't want…" Nana's voice faded away as she understood their subtleness to leave me and Campbell alone to talk. I watched them shuffle away, dad reaching for mum's hand as she led Nana back towards Sea Colme.

None of this made any sense! What was Campbell doing here? Why wasn't he keeping Sophie warm somewhere?

"Isla?"

I willed myself not to turn my head to look at Campbell. I was mad at him.

I felt his hand on my shoulder and I spun around to look at him. I really should tell him to back off before he pushed things too far.

As I turned, I saw he was holding a basket of red and white tablecloth garlands, stacks of panettone, and cannoli wrapped in gift-sized cellophane parcels.

I furrowed my brows.

"What are you doing here?" I blurted out.

Campbell looked down at his shoes. At least he had the decency to look ashamed!

"Things have changed." He said and my heart sank to my feet. "Quite a lot actually and I wanted it to be perfect when I finally told you," he said. "But I guess your Nana is right and there is no perfect time."

I looked up at him, his green eyes shining, his hair askew. Campbell did not look like his usual polished self. I couldn't even begin to make sense of what he was saying.

"I did it, Isla, I am giving it a try, just like you. I've given up the job with my dad," Campbell said, taking a deep breath. "And, I've followed my heart." He gave a lopsided smile and lifted the basket of tablecloths. "I opened my own business."

"It's you who bought Barnacles?" I said, my eyes wide with shock as everything fell into place.

"I did," he said with a huge smile.

"What about Sophie?" I said, thinking of what I had seen — the two of them laughing together outside the office building.

"Sophie?" Campbell furrowed his brows in confusion.

"I saw you with her, and I saw her here, in town." My voice pitched and fell, and Campbell must have heard the emotion behind my words.

He shook his head.

"She was helping my dad tie up some loose ends with the purchase..." He scratched his head. "But she has nothing to do with me, nor I her. To be perfectly honest, I'm not a huge fan of Sophie." He looked at me, his face expressionless. "I think she's a... a... cold fish."

I couldn't help but laugh at his description of my former manager, as relief washed over me.

"But I am a fan of you," Campbell said. "And I apologise for appearing and disappearing all the time, I've been so busy setting up the Deli, I haven't had a minute to myself."

I stared at Campbell, here in mum's Christmas market, his basket full of items for his stall, as I made sense of his words.

"This is a wonderful town, Isla, I feel so welcome. And, perhaps we can organise a real date, what about tomorrow?" Campbell sounded unsure. "I can promise that I'll be around here a lot more," he said.

I shook my head.

"I don't believe it," I said. "Won't you miss Edinburgh?"

It was Campbell's turn to shake his head.

"No, not one bit. It's amazing here, you said it yourself! It feels like home. Something I never really had." He smiled, and at that moment I felt my hesitations melt away.

"I will go on that date with you," I said. "But on one condition."

"Yes?" he said, his eyes shining.

"I'd like you to cook me dinner," I said.

"I'd love that. It's a date then." He smiled. "Finally."

"Finally," I agreed.

I don't know how long we stood there, staring at each other with our dopey smiles. It was probably only a few seconds, but it felt like forever.

"Treats ahoy!" Said a voice and I turned around and Mum was moving closer, holding a tray with two slices of Joyce's secret sinful recipe Christmas loaf, spread with butter and topped with apricot jam. Nana was tottering behind her.

"Oh, delicious, thanks, mum. I haven't had any of Joyce's cake yet," I said, reaching out a hand to take a slice. It wasn't just dad who enjoyed it.

"Thanks, Jan, delicious." Campbell took a slice of Christmas loaf.

"Mabel, you'll be pleased to know we've also set a dinner date," Campbell said looking from Nana to me. I tried to hide that my mouth was stuffed with Christmas loaf. "I have a question."

Nana suddenly looked suspicious.

"Do you?" she said, her eyes narrowing.

"I hear you need a hip operation," he said, "shall we talk about when you're going to book it." I smiled as Nana tried to protest but maybe she had finally met her match. Campbell turned to me and winked.

I left the two of them to bicker over dates and reasons not to get a new hip and dashed back to Sea Colme Cottage to get more boxes of buns for mum's stall. Mum was in the kitchen packing a box of cellophane parcels — Christmas cookies in the shape of trees, snowmen, and reindeer.

"So," she said. "Did the two of you make up? Nana told us you were sweet on each other but things were progressing slowly." I felt my face flush, and Mum reached out and patted my arm. "And, he not only has Nana's seal of approval, he also has ours."

"When did you meet him?" I was curious.

Mum grinned. "Hetty and Burt wanted me and Dad to meet him before they agreed to sell to him. They wanted to be sure about preserving the community spirit of the High Street. Campbell's plans are very entrepreneurial. And your Dad likes that he can play golf." Mum gave me a knowing look.

I laughed. Campbell had single-handedly charmed my family.

"He might even convince Nana to get her hip operation," Mum said with a raised eyebrow.

"I think he already has," I snorted.

25

The lights from the Christmas tree twinkled and shone as we sat on the beach, around the fire that dad built on this exact spot every year. My iPod blasted Christmas songs from the playlist dad had made especially for this night, and I hugged the blanket I was wrapped in a little closer around myself.

I'd realised over the last few months that a square peg shouldn't try to fit into a round hole. My life was here in this town, with my parents. It wasn't in Edinburgh trying to fit into someone else's life, not Tim's nor Mairi's. I was happier than I had been in months and as I looked across at Campbell, sitting alongside Nana and making sure her glass was kept topped up, I had an inkling that there might be more happiness in store for me.

There was something about Campbell that was special, he fit in here with my family and this life, he loved Charlie, he liked my parents, and he adored my Nana. He was perfect.

I caught Campbell's eyes and we smiled at each other. He whispered something in Nana's ear then came and sat beside me.

"What a night," he exclaimed as he sat down.

I rubbed my hands close to the fire.

"It's the best night of the year," I said, sitting back and leaning into Campbell's body for support. He looked up at the sky.

"It could be better," he said.

"Better?" I laughed, with an incredulous look on my face.

It had been a wonderful weekend for the Christmas market. Everyone had chatted and shopped, with bigger crowds than ever, and we'd been rushed off of our feet for hours. Most stalls had sold out. Everyone said they couldn't wait for next year so they could do it all over again.

Mairi had come to visit with her parents, and she'd bought gifts to hand out to her work colleagues. She was excited about the move to Milan, although her parents seemed sad, their faces a little strained. They adored Mairi and wanted her to be happy — if supporting her on this move was what they had to do, then they would do it.

The whole town had turned out in support of the local community, and it was heartwarming to see the stalls busy, and people standing around laughing with mugs of gluhwein and spiced hot chocolate. The air sparkled with Christmas spirit.

Even Johnny had turned up, with Pickles. He seemed to be back with his ex, and Sally shot me a look when they arrived — I knew there would be gossip to share.

He'd avoided mum's stall and I pretended I didn't know him, glad we didn't have to confront each other. I was also happy that at least we had seen each other in public. It should make the next meeting go even smoother.

It was almost a perfect night, and I realised what Campbell had meant when he said it could be better. This night needed to be sealed with a kiss.

I looked across at mum, dad and Nana, who were chatting on the other side of the fire with Sally and Caleb, and Sky McKay and her boyfriend, Joe. No one would miss us if we slipped away for a minute or two.

"Let's walk Charlie?" I said to Campbell, who stood up and dusted himself down immediately.

"Great idea," he said.

As soon as we were far enough away from the noise and light of the fire, Campbell turned to me. Charlie stopped and sat down at my heels, as I turned my face up towards Campbell.

He reached his hand up to brush my hair behind my ears. My chin was turned towards him and I caught the slightest glint of the fire in the distance reflected in his eyes.

"Perfect," he said, leaning forward to kiss me and I caught my breath.

He kissed me softly at first and then his hands were in my hair, and my hands were holding onto his neck and willing him to kiss me with more passion. His arms held me secure, as he tenderly planted kisses along my cheek. I shivered in anticipation of more of this, tonight and tomorrow and for the months and maybe even years to come. I wanted to grab Campbell's hand and take him to my room at Sea Colme Cottage so we could continue our kissing. Then he sighed.

"I've wanted to do this so much tonight," he whispered. "It was torture watching you and not being able to hold you."

I nuzzled my face into his neck, breathing in his scent.

"Me too," I admitted, I'd spent the night serving customers and stealing looks across at him. I didn't know how things would pan out, but I was delighted he had made a commitment to our town and he seemed to be on the same wavelength as me.

"I think you're beautiful," he said into my hair.

"You're pretty easy on the eye yourself," I said.

He laughed.

"I wanted to come and see you so many times, but something always came up. I've learned it takes a lot of time to run your own business."

I agreed with that. Running Sea Colme Cottage while mum and dad were away had given me new insight. It's incredible, the details, the things you have to remember.

"Perhaps we can learn from each other?" he said. "Your marketing skills would be helpful to me. If you're still keen on some freelance work?"

"I'd like that." I nuzzled deeper into his embrace. "I could stay here all night," I said.

"Me too." I could feel him nod, then felt him pull away. "But…"

"We should get back to everyone." I agreed.

We gazed deeply into each other's eyes, some words not needing to be said out loud. Then we turned and entwined our hands as we walked back towards the party.

That night my heart was bursting with love for everyone around me. Anything was possible, with Charlie at my heels, and Campbell's hand in mine.

I was sure this new adventure back home was just about to begin. And I would celebrate all of life's little wins.

Sinful Bakes Christmas Loaf Recipe

Christmas in Sea Colme Cottage wouldn't be Christmas without a slice of the sinful Christmas loaf. My dear friend, Sinem, of the popular @SinfulBakes and @Sinfluencer - I'm That Mum TikTok and Instagram accounts, has thankfully shared it here for us all to enjoy. I don't know about you, but my season got a lot yummier!

- 420 Grams of bread flour
- 300-320 ml Lukewarm water
- 7 grams of dried active yeast
- 1 Tsp salt
- 2 Tsp Sugar
- 2 Tsp Cinnamon
- 3 Tsp Mixed Spice
- 200 grams glacier cherries
- 250 grams of mixed dried fruit
- Add a few chopped dried figs and dates
- 100 grams of walnuts (optional)

1.   First put all of the dry ingredients together and make a well in the Center. Then fill the well with water. You may not need it all. If it's too dry then add more water, too sticky, and a little more flour. Once kneaded by

hand for 5-10 mins, (or using a hook attachment) place the dough in a deep bowl, cover it with a wet tea towel and leave it to rise in a warm place for 1 hour.

2. Once risen, punch the dough down and add all of the fruit and nuts (if using). It's a messy job but totally worth it.

3. Shape it into a loaf and put it on the tray you intend for the oven. Cover with a tea towel and leave to rise for another hour.

4. Once risen, brush with milk and sprinkle with cinnamon sugar.

5. Bake in a preheated oven @160fan/180c for 30 minutes

6. Serve with chopped chunky cheddar and Apricot Jam!

Keep up with Sinful Bakes on Instagram or TikTok!

ABOUT THE AUTHOR

Karlie Parker is from London but currently lives in Edinburgh with her husband, children and pups. She is the author of the Sea Colme Cottage Series, and The Yoga Retreat due 2023. She has an unhealhty obsession with Bravo's Real Housewives franchises and scandi buns! Follow her on Instagram @iamstillkarlie or TikTok @iamstillkarliee or her website www.karlieparker.com

Printed in Great Britain
by Amazon

30976835R00086